**His c...
stirr...**

"I have a rule." Enrico trailed his fingers through her hair. "I don't make love to women who don't want to."

"I didn't say I don't want to. Not many ever say no, I expect."

He gave a crooked smile. "I haven't made love to many women."

Chantal laughed softly. "That's not a very macho statement, you know. Are you sure you're half Brazilian?"

"Quite. But when I do anything, I do it right, or at least I try. When I'm involved, I'm involved. I don't go for fast flings and one-night stands, so you'd better be prepared."

"What exactly should I be prepared for?" she asked.

"To take this relationship seriously," he said. "To take my feelings for you seriously."

KAREN VAN DER ZEE is an author on the move. Her husband's work as an agricultural advisor to developing countries has taken them to many exotic locations. The couple said their marriage vows in Kenya, celebrated the birth of their first daughter in Ghana and their second in the United States, where they make their permanent home. The whole family spent two fascinating years in Indonesia. Karen has had several short stories published in her native Holland, and her modern romance novels with their strong characters and colorful backgrounds are enjoyed around the world.

Books by Karen van der Zee

HARLEQUIN PRESENTS

HARLEQUIN ROMANCE

Don't miss any of our special offers. Write to us at the following address for information on our newest releases.

Harlequin Reader Service
901 Fuhrmann Blvd., P.O. Box 1397, Buffalo, NY 14240
Canadian address: P.O. Box 603,
Fort Erie, Ont. L2A 5X3

KAREN
VAN DER ZEE

brazilian fire

Harlequin Books

TORONTO • NEW YORK • LONDON
AMSTERDAM • PARIS • SYDNEY • HAMBURG
STOCKHOLM • ATHENS • TOKYO • MILAN

Harlequin Presents first edition November 1989
ISBN 0-373-11222-X

Original hardcover edition published in 1989
by Mills & Boon Limited

CHAPTER ONE

RIVER of January. Such a strange name for a city, Chantal thought as she pushed her bacon around on her plate. Rio de Janeiro. It had the ring of romance and adventure and it would be wonderful to go there, to put the last few horrible months behind her. To figure out what to do with the rest of her life.

The rest of her life.

A barren stretch of emptiness.

Rain streamed down the kitchen window and a stormy wind lashed the trees, sending showers of coloured leaves flying. Autumn. Winter coming. In Brazil it was spring, warm enough to go to the beach in Rio—Ipanema Beach. Chantal sighed with longing and tossed her hair back over her shoulder. She glanced at her sister across from her. Sleepy-eyed, blonde hair all tangled, Dominique nibbled at her toast with distaste.

'I want you to come back to Rio with me,' she said in French. Dominique spoke English only when absolutely necessary. '*Maman* insists I bring you back. No reason to stay in this pathetic little hick town.'

Chantal regarded her sister with irritation. Dominique was blonde, beautiful, spoiled and a snob. She had married a Brazilian, had a baby and been divorced all in the space of eighteen months. 'There's nothing wrong with Perrydale, Dominique. I was born here. I've lived here all my life. You were born here too, remember?'

Dominique rolled her eyes. 'I don't want to remember,

chérie.' She laughed. 'Anyway, come to Rio. Rio is marvellous, and you'll love the Palácio.'

No reason to stay on in Perrydale. No, not really. Grief overwhelmed Chantal and she swallowed hard. Dad was dead. And he had always been the only reason for her to live in Perrydale, Illinois, rather than with her mother and sister in France. She had loved her father. She was her father's daughter, and after her parents' divorce she had stayed with him, while her sister had gone back to France with their high-society French mother who had never adjusted to being the wife of a country doctor in a rural American town.

No reason to stay on in Perrydale. Four months ago she had broken with David. Four days ago Dad had died of a heart attack. Too much loss in too short a time-span. She closed her eyes, forcing back the pain. *Don't think,* she thought. *Don't think.*

She had lived in Perrydale all of her twenty-seven years, but she had never truly belonged. She was an oddity in this small country town, having a French mother and spending every summer in the South of France with her wealthy French family. She was more sophisticated than her peers, more travelled, and she spoke fluent French. She had a strange foreign name and she was quiet and withdrawn and she played the piano better than anyone else in town. She looked different with her rich, sable brown hair and pale green eyes and beautiful clothes from Paris. Her father was the only doctor for miles around, loved and respected by all, but the kids thought Chantal was stuck-up and a snob.

Dominique pushed her plate back with a grimace of disgust. 'When are the Americans ever going to learn to bake decent bread?' she said irritably.

'They probably like their bread the way it is.'

'That's because they don't know any better.'

'Oh, for God's sake, Dominique! What does it matter?'

'It matters a great deal. I like good food. I like good coffee at breakfast. I thought you were French enough to agree with that.'

What mattered was that Dominique got everything the way she wanted it. All her life she'd had everything the way she wanted it. Except maybe her marriage.

'I think that none of it is very important considering the circumstances. As you may recall, we buried our father yesterday. Granted, he was American, and not French, but . . .'

'Don't be nasty, *chérie*. Let's just pack up and get out of here. We can get the first plane out tomorrow.'

Chantal suppressed a sigh. Dominique was not used to giving much consideration to anything beyond her own wishes and desires. 'I told you I can't leave just like that, Dominique. I have to deal with Dad's will, the lawyers, the practice, the house. I have commitments, responsibilities. I have a job. I took a few days off, but I can't just quit.'

'Why not? You don't need that job. It's always been a mystery to me why you worked at all. Let them find someone else, and I'm sure the lawyers are perfectly capable of handling Dad's affairs on their own. Tell them what you want, give them power of attorney and off you go. Simple.'

Chantal could feel the anger bubbling up again. 'Dominique, you may not understand this, but . . .'

Dominique came to her feet and waved her elegant hand in dismissal. 'Oh, for heaven's sake, spare me! I'm going to get dressed.'

Chantal poured herself another cup of coffee and walked forlornly through the house, not knowing what to do or where to begin. It would take days to pack up. She wondered how long they would need to find another manager at the inn, or at least a temporary solution. Even her job wasn't worth staying for, not any more at least. Ever since the new owner had taken over the inn, Chantal had known nothing but frustration.

Dominique was right. There was nothing worth staying for. She would got to Rio, stay at the Palácio and laze on the beach. She needed the break. She was exhausted. She'd worked too hard, too long after the break-up with David. Anything to block out the anger and anguish, anything so she wouldn't have to think. She closed her eyes, fighting a hopeless longing, resting her forehead against the cool glass of the window. 'Oh, David,' she whispered, 'why did you do that to me? Now that I need you, I can't have you. Why did you deceive me so?'

She pushed the thoughts away, trying not to remember the pain in his eyes, trying only to remember the rage she had felt. Yet all she saw where his eyes, the despair in his face.

'I love you,' he had said, 'and I'll be back for you.'

'Don't you ever come back! I *never* want to see you again! How could you? How *could* you do this to me? I gave you everything—my love, my trust, and you *lied* to me! You *deceived* me!'

She had loved him with all her heart. She felt betrayed, enraged, stupid.

And scared to have been fooled so completely.

Dominique, dressed and gorgeous, swept into the room. She had the knack of looking perfectly casual in the most elegant way. Wearing narrow black trousers, high black boots and a bright red belted tunic of soft wool, she did just that. Chantal studied her sister dispassionately. Smooth cap of shiny gold hair, large, baby-blue eyes that looked not at all innocent, full red mouth. She was beautiful, and with her pale hair no doubt got a lot of attention in Brazil. She wondered how long it wold take her sister to find another husband.

'Not a Brazilian, at least. Not in a million years,' Dominique had stated once, her voice hard and bitter. 'Brazilian men give the word male chauvinist new meaning.'

Yet she still lived in Rio with her little daughter. Probably because their mother had followed suit and married a Brazilian as well a few months later and now lived in Rio with her husband, Matteus Moreyra, who owned the Hotel Palácio on Ipanema Beach, as well as several others around the world.

Chantel gestured around the room. 'Dominique, is there anything you want from the house, anything of Dad's?'

'What could I possibly want?'

'I don't know. But this was your father's house, your home for the first ten years of your life. Maybe there's something in the attic, some toys. Something you might want to give to Nicole.'

'I'm not going to crawl around in some dusty attic. I can't imagine what I would possibly want.' She scanned the room with mild distaste. 'Why didn't you ever do something about this place, Chantal? The furniture, the . . .'

'There's nothing wrong with the furniture.'

'It's so tacky and middle class.'

'I am tacky and middle class. Dad was tacky and middle class. We like tacky and middle class. You're such a damn snob, Dominique.'

Dominique laughed. 'And you're so touchy. And wrong. There's nothing tacky about you, Chantal. Look in the mirror. You're beautiful. People would kill for your hair and those gorgeous green eyes. You should get yourself some decent clothes, though. You used to love good clothes. Remember how we used to go shopping in Paris together?'

'I still like good clothes, and yes, I do remember.'

'We'll go shopping when you come to Rio. I know just the places to go.'

No doubt she did. Dominique spent half her waking life shopping and she had never done a day's work in her life.

'I wish I could stay on and help you,' Dominique said, 'but I've got to go back home. I've got to get back to Nicole.'

'I imagine *Maman* and your nanny are taking care of her quite adequately.

'I'm sure they are. But I've never left her before.' Dominique smiled, and the softness in her blue eyes made her suddenly seem younger and less worldly. 'I miss her,' she said softly. 'Without her my days just don't seem right.'

Rio de Janeiro was beautiful. From her seat near the window Chantal had a perfect view as the plane circled and slowly made its descent. The city hugged the green hills surrounding the bay with its many inlets and long stretches of white beaches. High on a mountain peak towered the imposing statue of Christ the Redeemer, arms stretched out in blessing over the city.

Dominique was waiting for her at the gate, casually elegant inn a slip of a white dress that no doubt had cost hundreds of dollars. She hugged her in warm welcome. 'I'm glad you're here.' She stood back and frowned at Chantal's pale yellow warm-up suit and white running shoes. 'Didn't you have anything better to wear? You look as if you're on the way to the jogging track.'

'I was very comfortable, and that's all I care about when I have to spend an entire night on a plane.'

Dominique shrugged. 'You're hopeless, *chérie*. Let's go.

We have a limousine waiting.'

A limousine. Chantal smiled at herself as she followed her sister out of the terminal, a uniformed man carrying her two suitcases.

The limousine had soft velvet upholstery and was fitted with a wet bar, soft drinks, ice and a small TV. 'Whose car is this?'

'The hotel's. Specially for famous and important guests.'

'I'm impressed.'

'Wait till you see the hotel.' Dominique leaned forward and opened the small refrigerator. 'So, how about a glass of champagne to celebrate?'

'Champagne? At nine in the morning?'

Dominique grinned. 'What else at nine in the morning?'

'How about a cup of coffee? *Café au lait* would be perfect.'

'God, you're a spoilsport.'

It was not a long ride to Ipanema. All along the beach, the buildings were tall and narrow, due to lack of space and the high price of beach-front property. Chantal had seen pictures of the Hotel Palàcio, but the reality was even more impressive. Thirty-two storeys of sleek contemporary design towered into the sky. The limousine made a smooth stop in front of the main entrance and the door was opened immediately by the uniformed doorman sporting a welcoming smile.

The soft, rushing sound of falling water greeted Chantal as she stepped through the doors of the hotel. An enormous fountain graced the middle of the vast, marble-floored lobby. She stood for a moment, staring up at the sparkling water as it cascaded down in eternal fall.

'Good lord,' she said to Dominique, 'just looking at this ought to cool you off when you come in from the beach.'

'Dramatic, isn't it?'

'I'd say so.' She glanced around, taking in the enormous palms and lush flowering plants, the chandeliers, the giant tapestries on the walls, the people milling about. Then she noticed the man striding purposefully towards them.

'Oh, no,' muttered Dominique, 'here comes Mr High and Mighty.'

The man approached them across the cool marble floor, dark and tall and imposing, wearing an impeccable black suit.

'Welcome to the Palácio, Ms Stevenson. I'm Enrico Chamberlain, the general manager. We were expecting you.' He held out his hand and Chantal looked into the coldest, greyest eyes she had ever seen.

He emanated a kind of power, a magnetism. Here was a man with an iron will who bent to nothing and nobody. There was a moment of silence as their eyes locked and she felt a shiver go down her spine. Everything about him spelled perfection and control. The face—angular, handsome, carved out of stone; the black suit, tailored to perfection; the pose, full of arrogant self-confidence.

He grasped her hand in a quick, firm grip and released it instantly. He nodded coolly to Dominique. 'Good morning, Senhora Hilvares.' His gaze swept back to Chantal. There was mockery in his eyes, a hint of contempt she did not understand. She glanced back at Dominique, whose face had turned stony and expressionless. She had never seen her sister look like that.

'I hear you're joining the rest of the family,' Enrico Chamberlain said, the hard eyes assessing her. His English was unmistakably New England and his voice carried a tone of barely disguised disapproval. Chantal had learned from her father to listen to what was not being said, to hear the meaning hidden behind the spoken words. It was clear to her, if not to anyone else, that this handsome stranger, this man she had never set eyes on, did not like her here and did not welcome her.

'For a while, yes,' she said politely, wondering what was going on, why this man eyed her with such dislike. He made her uneasy, made her feel on the defensive without even knowing against what she was defending herself. He made her feel small and insignificant, and all her defences rallied in that one moment of contact.

'I hope you'll be comfortable,' he remarked, sounding as if he didn't care a hoot if she were or not.

'If I'm not comfortable at the Palácio, where would I be?' she answered lightly.

'Indeed.' His face was inscrutable. 'Let me know if there is anything you need or want.'

'That's very kind of you, but I'm sure I can make do with Housekeeping or the Director of Guest Relations.'

One dark brow raised. 'You are not a mere paying guest, Ms Stevenson.'

No, she was an non-paying one. The hotel-owner's stepdaughter. She regarded him evenly. It was important not to let him notice her thoughts. 'Meaning?'

'If there are any problems at all, please let me know personally.' His tone held dismissal and he glanced swiftly at his thin gold watch. 'I hope you will find your suite in order. I'll see you at the cocktail party tonight.'

'Thank you.' She watched the broad back retreat, then turned to Dominique.

'What's the matter with him?'

Dominique waved her hands, her frozen face relaxing. 'Who knows. He's an arrogant son of a bitch. Uncle

Matteus's *Wunderkind*. There was a big shake-up a few years ago and the GM got fired and Uncle Matteus hired Chamberlain away from some classy hotel in Geneva.'

'And is he good?'

'Very, very good,' she said drily, 'if you listen to Uncle Matteus.'

'Is he American?'

'Half. His mother is Brazilian.'

'He sounds very New England.'

'Boston, Harvard.'

Chantal grimaced. 'Oh, of course.' It explained something—the inbred arrogance and self-possession of generations of money and power and influence—if not everything. It did not explain the dislike she had seen in the icy depths of the grey eyes.

A private lift took them to the princely penthouse apartment on the top floor where her mother and Uncle Matteus spent part of the year. It was lavishly appointed, like everything else in the hotel. Chantal recognised some of her mother's furniture from France, some exquisite antiques, a large Persian carpet in jewelled colours, oil paintings, a lamp.

Her mother had not changed since the last time Chantal had seen her, almost two years earlier at her grandparents' villa on Cap d'Antibes. Her mother didn't seem to age. She was as beautiful and youthful as ever. Even her perfume was the same, Chantal realised as she hugged her.

Two years. *How could it be that I haven't seen my mother in two years?*

Uncle Matteus kissed her warmly on the cheek. He was of medium height, dark but greying, and not particularly handsome in the traditional sense, but there was about him an aura of power, of effortless command.

'Please be assured that I am very happy to have you here with us. Consider this your home,' he said, dark eyes smiling. 'As long as you'll let me introduce you as my daughter.'

'Thank you,' she said, touched by his generosity.

Her mother took her hand. 'You must be very tired, *chérie*.'

'Exhausted. I couldn't sleep on the plane.'

'Well, I'm so glad you're here now, even though it was not happiness that finally made you come.' Her mother smiled at her with warmth and concern. 'I'm very sorry about your father, Chantal. And Dominique told me about David. You've not had an easy time lately, have you?'

'No'. Chantal felt a choking sensation. Something broke inside her. Maybe it was Uncle Matteus's kindness, or the concern in her mother's eyes. Her legs began to tremble. I'm just tired, she told herself, I was flying all night. Tears burned behind her eyes, then welled up and blinded her.

She groped for a chair and sat down, covering her face. She had held on to her composure for too long. 'I'm sorry, I'm sorry,' she cried, mortified at her sudden loss of control.

'*Chérie!* What's wrong!'

Chantal shook her head. 'I'm just tired.'

But it wasn't just physical fatigue. It was much more than that. It was her heart and her soul and the pain and loss of the past months . . . David, her father.

She cried until she had no tears left.

She stayed in bed for the rest of the day, passing the hours in exhausted sleep. She awoke in the late afternoon, knowing she would sleep no more, yet not feeling refreshed. It felt as if she were going to be tired for the rest of her life, a weariness of the soul that seemed unrelieved by sleep.

She stretched in the king-size bed, savouring the feel of the cool sheets against her skin, and surveyed the bedroom. The carpeting was deep and soft, the colour of pale jade, the same shade as the upholstered chairs. Original artwork decorated the wall. A single pink rose in a silver bud-vase graced the bedside table.

She had her own suite of rooms—a large bedroom, a palatial sitting-room with arched windows that overlooked the glistening green-blue ocean, the wide, curved beach and the hills beyond. Exquisite furniture with overstuffed cushions, large potted palms and an exotic flower arrangement were part of the luxurious décor. There was a small bar, a refrigerator and a colour TV set in both the sitting-room and the bedroom. A large basket of fresh fruit stood on the table—perfect, blushing mangoes, s small papaya, bananas, red apples.

The bathroom was a dream of pale pink marble, a sunken tub, soft Turkish towels, and bottles and jars of Guerlain toiletries. A white terry-cloth bathrobe hung behind the door. There was an adjoining dressing-room with an entire wall of cupboard space, floor-to-ceiling mirrors and an antique dressing-table worth a fortune.

In this place of grace and luxury, she would want for nothing. She smiled at nothing in particular. It felt good to be here. The luxury was comforting.

She glanced at the bedside clock. Ten to six. The cocktail party was at seven in her mother's penthouse apartment. The last thing she wanted was to get up, dress and go to a party where she would have to be charming to strangers. But the party was for her, to introduce her to her mother and stepfather's circle of friends, a gesture of kindness. The lost daughter, finally returned home, needed new friends, new people to socialise with.

Enrico Chamberlain. She grimaced as her mind produced a picture of the handsome face with the hard, strong features, the square chin, and the steely eyes. Enrico Chamberlain would be at the party. She wondered what was the matter with the man and why he didn't like her. It might be interesting to find out. Maybe. Remembering the scornful grey eyes, she felt the unease creep through her again. The man was unnerving and she had no idea why. She shrugged it off, swinging her legs out of bed, and made her way into the pink marble bathroom.

The party was like many she had attended in France—a room full of bright, beautiful people, drinking and laughing and secretly studying each other. Women in designer clothes—Givenchy, Yves St Laurent, Ungaro. The air was fragrant with perfume—Chanel No. 5, Capucci de Capucci, Arpège.

'You look lovely, *chérie*,' her mother said, surveying her simple green dress, 'but isn't this just a bit . . . modest?'

'Understated, *Maman*. I think that's the term.'

Her mother gave an amused half-smile. 'Well, yes. I suppose understatement always was your style.'

Introductions were made. There was a coffee baron, an olive king, and African princess in fuchsia feathers, an Italian model in a jazzy little dress of red gauze and lace. Chantal shook hands, smiled, looked gracious.

'I *love* New York,' the model confided, having just returned from there. 'It's so *active*, so full of energy. I always feel so *alive*, so *charged* when I'm there.'

'It's too cold,' the princess commented. Her hair was an elaborate construction of plaits and beads and feathers. In the bizarre feather dress she looked like some exotic jungle bird. 'I much prefer Rome or Rio.' She also preferred nude beaches, big diamonds, and chocolates from Lenotre in Paris.

Chantal listened, saying little. At social affairs she always enjoyed listening more than talking.

There was a parade of handsome young men who all wanted to talk to her—a prominent architect, a famous photographer, a stockbroker and a variety of business types who had made it rich in minerals or hardwood or real estate.

She made small talk in French and English, slowly sipping a glass of white wine, and wondered why her sister had not made an appearance, and what had happened to Mr General Manager. May he wouldn't make if after all. Just as well.

No such luck. She noticed him as soon as he entered the room, wearing an elegant dark suit. He stood still for a moment, surveying the room and the people in it with an arrogant, imperious tilt of his head and a vaguely mocking expression on his face.

Chantal turned and went in search of her mother. 'Where's Dominique? I haven't seen her.'

'She's just telephoned. She has a terrible headache.'

Chantel met her mother's eyes. Her sister was famous for her convenient headaches. Chantal wondered why Dominique didn't want to be at the cocktail party.

'Have you two been arguing?' her mother asked.

'Arguing? For heaven's sake, *Maman*, no.'

Her mother frowned, then shrugged lightly.'Well, I have no idea what's the matter with her.' Her face brightened. 'Oh, here is Enrico.' She put her hand on his arm. Good to see you. Talk to my daughter, will you? I must see to my other guests.' She glided away with a rustle of ivory silk.

Enrico inclined his head slightly, his eyes sweeping over

her in quick appraisal. 'Good evening, Ms Stevenson.

'Good evening, Mr Chamberlain.'

'Have you recuperated from your flight?' he asked, cool eyes not reflecting his smile.

'I hope so.' She sipped her drink. This was going to be one of those excruciatingly polite little conversations, she could tell. She braced herself. He's not going to get to me, she told herself. I'm going to be perfectly self-possessed if it kills me. Her defence mechanisms were revving up to full steam.

'Did you find everything in order in your rooms?'

'I couldn't be more comfortable, thank you.'

'We strive to please.'

'And I hear you're very good at it.' Oh, God, she thought, regretting the words instantly. It sounded like a double-entendre, which she had not at all intended. She kept her face as cool as she could manage under his keen regard. For a moment his grey eyes held hers.

'Oh?'

'You're Uncle Matteus's *Wunderkind*, I'm told. His right hand, his left.'

His face was carefully bland. 'I wonder who told you that.'

'It wouldn't be very discreet of me to tell you, would it?'

He gave a crooked little smile. 'No, probably not. Have you ever been to Rio before, Ms Stevenson?'

The formality was killing her. Ms Stevenson. Good lord. Well, she wasn't going to suggest he call her Chantal. 'No, I have not, but I understand it's a beautiful, exciting city.'

'As you will no doubt find out very soon.' He smiled charmingly. Nothing in his voice gave away the underlying sarcasm, yet she sensed it was there.

What was going on here? she asked herself. She didn't

like this man. She observed him silently, not answering, and he smiled again. 'I'm sure your mother and sister have planned to keep you busy, go to the right places, introduce you to the right people.'

'Right people? As opposed to wrong people? You've got those in Brazil too?' She frowned with mock concern. 'Oh dear, I hope it isn't too hard to know the difference. It's so awkward in a foreign country.'

It was the first time she saw a glint of humour in the grey eyes. 'I'm sure your instincts are superbly tuned. Not to worry.'

She would have gladly poured her drink over his thirty-dollar haircut. Instead, she took a careful sip and glanced around the room. 'To start with, I suppose I should circulate and talk to some more of the right people.' She smiled up at him. 'If you'll excuse me?'

He inclined his head and she moved away, feeling his eyes on her back. To hell with him, she thought, annoyed with herself for feeling disturbed by him.

During the course of the evening, she received a number of propositions and invitations. The coffee baron offered to educate her and show her his coffee plantations. The stockbroker invited her to dinner so that he could tell her about some very interesting stock he knew of. The lawyer suggested a night-time stroll on the beach.

By one in the morning she had had enough and slipped away, back to the big, comfortable bed in the large, quiet suite.

For the next three days she slept and cried and slept some more. Physically and emotionally she felt wiped out. She did not leave her rooms, but gratefully submitted to the tender ministrations of her mother and sister. She was not very hungry, but the food was tempting, delicious fruits, fresh breads and the best the hotel had to offer.

Her sleep was fitful, full of restless images flitting through her mind—mixed up visions of Dad and David and Enrico, of medical emergencies, of Enrico telling her he loved her. Or was it David? Faces, voices blurred, faded. Dad, dog-tired, coming in late after having dealt with an emergency, saying he wanted her to come back to Perrydale because David was in the hospital.

Sitting up in bed, she watched movies on the hotel video and slept some more. She had never slept so much in her life. She had never cried so much in her life. She couldn't make herself stop. The pain had been held in too long, stored away, until it had finally come rushing out like a waterfall tumbling over a ledge. Her mother worried. Dominique worried. She was beginning to worry herself.

'It's not just Dad, is it?' Dominique demanded. 'You're crying for that louse David, right? Well, that's men for you, *chérie*. They're not to be trusted. I simply do not understand how you could be so naïve. You're such an innocent!'

Chantal resented being called naïve. She was neither naïve nor innocent. David had been exceedingly clever. She didn't like being naïve, but she certainly didn't want to be a cynic like her sister. She wanted to love a man, trust him, and not be suspicious, worrying about possible affairs and other betrayals.

So, maybe she was naïve.

After several days she was beginning to feel better. Sleep restored her, physically at least, maybe emotionally as well. David wasn't worthy of her misery and her father wouldn't want her to cry herself sick over his death. Go on with your life, he would say.

She wondered what she was going to do with herself. No job, no house to take care off. Nobody expected anything of her. She had no goals, no dreams. Her dreams had been taken away by David, a brutal disillusionment she would not forget easily.

On Thursday afternoon, Enrico paid her a visit. She had expected it to be her mother or her sister knocking on the door, and she stared at him a little stupidly as he entered the room at her invitation. She was sitting cross-legged on the big bed, still wearing her nightgown, watching a movie and painting her toenails. She was aware of the fact that she didn't make the most elegant of pictures, even though her nightgown was a chic, sensuous affair of silk and lace—a gift from her mother—and she was irrationally angry at him for coming to see her in this state of undress, her hair a mess, her face devoid of make-up. It made her feel vulnerable. With a man like Enrico you wanted to look your best so that you could feel on top of things. It was infinitely easier to face a man like Enrico Chamberlain while dressed in lace and diamonds. Right now she was in no shape to see anybody, least of all Enrico with his arrogant face.

The arrogant face studied her silently, one eyebrow cocked, then his gaze dropped to her feet. 'Beautiful colour,' he stated. 'Beautiful toes.'

'Thank you, Mr Chamberlain.' At least he was original. Nobody had ever complimented her on her toes. Her face, yes. Her eyes, her hair, her hands, yes. But not her toes.

His mouth twitched. 'It has been brought to my attention that you have kept yourself locked up in your rooms now for a number of days and I've come to see if there is anything we can do for you. Do you need a doctor, perhaps? Or a psychiatrist? Rio is very well stocked in that department.' His face was glacially polite.

A psychiatrist. The gall! The audacity! Well, he wasn't going to rile her, though God only knew why he wanted to. She tilted her head, pretending to consider his offer.

'I suppose there's a therapist you can recommend personally?'

'At the Palácio we only recommend the best,' he said smoothly, not missing a beat.

'Of course.' She twisted the bottle of nail polish between her fingers and frowned. 'Actually, I think a good hairdresser will do. Cheaper too.' She smiled sweetly.

'I can arrange that.'

'I wasn't serious.'

'Actually, I didn't think so. May I ask why you're in hiding?'

'I'm not in hiding and if I were it wouldn't be any of your business and now kindly get out of here, Mr Chamberlain, so I can finish painting my nails.'

'By all means, don't let me hold you up. I was merely checking up on the comforts of one of our most valued guests. I'm pleased to find you painting rather than pining.'

'You sound like an advertising brochure.'

His hand reached out for the door knob. 'Tempting, I hope?'

'No, full of platitudes and lacking in imagination.'

The grey eyes glittered briefly, with humour or anger, she couldn't tell. Then he opened the door and was gone.

CHAPTER TWO

THIS is heaven, Chantal thought, as she lay on a poolside lounger sipping a glass of grapefruit juice. Close, anyway. She smiled up at the sky. Thirty-odd storeys up from the ground. Who had ever heard of a roof-top swimming pool? The view of the sea and the hills certainly was magnificent.

Large, leafy plants and flowering bushes framed the outer edges of the roof and lounge chairs and small tables were placed around the pool. The pool shared the roof with a solarium which every morning was the scene of a lavish breakfast buffet. Businessmen and tourists alike enjoyed their morning coffee in the green, tropical ambience.

A shadow fell cross her bare legs. 'Ah, the body beautiful,' came a familiar voice.

Glancing up, Chantal met Enrico's cool grey gaze. His eyes travelled leisurely along the full length of her body in the skimpy, pale green swimsuit. She felt a tightening of her stomach. Anger, resentment, something else. She closed her eyes and ignored him. If he wanted to be offensive she would not satisfy him with a response.

'I am glad you've found your way out of your suite,' he said soothingly. 'I was beginning to worry.'

I'll bet, she thought. She opened her eyes and glared at him, saying nothing. He was wearing that damn dark suit again, complete with waistcoat and silk tie, and looked out of place, though strikingly handsome just the same. Possibly more so because of the contrast with the other near-naked bodies around the pool. She wondered what he would look like in some other outfit—tennis shorts, swimming-trunks. Nothing. She had a sudden vision of the tall, lean body in the shower. Soapsuds all over. Water streaming down a smooth, muscular back. Dark, wet hair clinging to the broad forehead. Maybe he sang in the shower. Great, she thought derisively, I'm progressing nicely.

She didn't like the way he was looking at her, as if he secretly mocked her. She wondered why this instant antagonism. She had never met him before; why was he treating her with this polite contempt?

'Be careful not to burn,' he commented. 'If you need some lotion, I can have it brought up to you.'

'I'm not an imbecile,' she snapped, 'and I can find my own lotion.' She sat up. 'Aren't you overdoing the solicitous bit just a trifle? Don't you have anything better to do than worry about my comfort?'

His nostrils flared and something sprang alive and the cool depths of his eyes. 'For God's sake, woman,' he muttered fiercely, 'don't be so damned stupid! It's winter in North America and your skin hasn't felt the sun for months! You're going to burn to a crisp sitting here at ten in the morning!'

Chantal felt a mixture of surprise and glee. Well, well, under all that New England ice there lurked some Brazilian fire. How very interesting.

'I'll be very careful,' she said soothingly. 'And thank you for your concern. *Muito obrigada*.' She smiled sweetly and she saw his jaw harden. Then his face smoothed out again in a cool mask. He had himself under control again. It must be hard, she thought, to have to deal with fire and ice at the same time.

He reached into his pocket and took out a folded piece of paper. 'For you,' he said, handing it to her. 'I happened to be in the office when it came in on the telex.'

Frowning, Chantal took the paper from him and opened it. 'I KNOW WHAT YOU ARE UP TO. DON'T THINK YOU CAN GET AWAY WITH IT.' It was signed *M*.

She stared at the paper, dumbfounded. It made no sense. She had not the vaguest notion what the message meant. She glanced up at Enrico.

'I don't think this is for me. I have no idea what this is about.'

'It's addressed to you,' he pointed out patiently.

And so it was. She stared at her name and the telex code of the hotel. There were more codes and numbers, but nothing that indicated the place of origin by name. 'I can't even tell where this is from.'

'It's in code. I'll find out.' The shadow shifted as he turned away. 'And have a pleasant day, Ms Stevenson.' He strode off, through the vine-covered archway into the solarium.

The next morning she awoke early and she knew she could no longer stay in bed. She ached to get out. It was only six thirty and the light outside was new and fresh, a clear spring morning. I'm better, she thought, feeling suddenly jubilantly happy. She pulled on her swimsuit and a white sarong-type wrap and slipped into white leather thongs. The beach, the ocean. Suddenly she couldn't wait to get outside and have a swim in the salty water, to hear the rushing of the waves and feel the sand between her toes.

No one else would be up. Her mother slept late, always, as did Dominique, who lived in her own apartment not far from the Palácio. Life for them did not begin until about noon, with a mad dash of lunches and fittings and shopping sprees and visits to galleries and showrooms, to be followed by drinks and dinner parties, all of which so far Chantal had avoided by staying in her room.

The hotel seemed deserted. Few people were out at this hour and she slipped out of the doors and crossed the Avenida Atlantica to the quiet beach. She dropped her towel in the sand and stretched, reaching for the blue sky, smiling, feeling a sudden glorious well-being.

'David,' she said out loud, 'I've cried enough. This is it. No more.'

The water was frigid, and she shivered a little, then splashed determinedly forward and dived straight into an oncoming wave.

The cold was exhilarating. She felt alive, more alive than she had felt for weeks and months, and she almost laughed out loud as she swam and splashed around in the cold water.

She stood upright, for a moment, to wipe the hair out of her eyes, when she noticed the jogger running along the beach.

Enrico. She recognised the face, the arrogant set of his chin, and unaccountably her pulse quickened. He wore blue running shorts and a sleeveless shirt and looked strong and athletic. His face was damp with perspiration and his hair lay limply across his forehead. He appeared infinitely more human than the cold man in the dark suit she knew in the hotel. His body was tall and lean, with wide shoulders, a hard, flat stomach and long, muscular legs. He moved with grace and ease and she knew she was staring as he ran past her. He didn't see her, his eyes focused straight ahead on something in the distance. She watched him go, slowly releasing her breath. There was no doubt that Enrico Chamberlain had one of the most virile, attractive bodies she had ever seen.

She dived back into the water and swam behind the breakers until finally she tired herself and let the waves roll her back to shore.

After breakfast at the rooftop solarium she explored the hotel, browsed through the bookshop and the little boutique selling bikinis and other beachwear. She checked out the health club and decided to come back later and have a work out.

She passed the deserted cocktail bar, the silent piano, and stopped. There was no one there. Not until early evening would anyone come here for drinks and to listen to the painist. The place was immaculate, the tables clean, the deep comfortable chairs carefully arranged. She walked up to the piano, her feet sinking away in the soft carpeting. She felt strange—as if she were trespassing in forbidden territory, which was absurd and she smiled a little at the idea. Her fingers itched to touch the keys. Guiltily, she lifted the lid and slid her fingers gently along the smooth, white keys. Then she relaxed and sat down on the stool. There was no music, but it didn't matter. There were pieces she knew by heart.

She played, forgetting everything, losing all sense of time.

It was almost an hour and a half later when she finally stopped, looking up, feeling almost dazed. She closed the lid and came to her feet. She felt relaxed and serene. She had missed playing, she realised. It had always been a way for her to get rid of her tensions, to make the world go away.

Back in her room she found a handwritten message from Enrico. *Telex code indicates origin of telex is Minneapolis, Minnesota.*

Minneapolis. She didn't know anyone in Minneapolis.

Enrico was ruining her mood and the pleasure she found in the comfort of her life at the hotel. She wanted to relax, to enjoy the lack of responsibility for a short time, to come to terms with her losses.

It was hard to relax when Enrico seemed determined to show up unexpectedly at any time of the day. He enquired if she was comfortable. If she wanted a guide to tour the city. He personally delivered messages from Uncle Matteus. He informed her of a special concert in town. Sometimes he would join the family for dinner or lunch. She would listen to Uncle Matteus and Enrico discussing business.

Now and then, as they ate, he would ask her polite questions. How did she like the food at the Palácio? Was the health club up to standard? Had she enjoyed the party the previous evening? She was aware of his scrutiny, as if he were studying her like some laboratory animal.

He was getting on her nerves.

'What is the matter with you and Enrico?' her mother asked one afternoon after another nerve-racking lunch. 'What is all that tension between you two?'

'I don't know,' she said, shrugging. 'The man doesn't like me.'

'Now why wouldn't he like you?'

'I wish I knew. He is cold and hopelessly polite and he drives me crazy'

Her mother frowned. 'Well, he isn't the *warmest* man I've ever known, but . . . aren't you imagining it?'

'No, I'm not imagining it.'

Her mother leaned back in her chair and sighed. 'He's a strange one, Enrico. I can't quite figure him out. He's a very private man and one never hears any talk about him or his . . . um, pursuits.'

'Women, you mean?'

Her mother nodded. 'Yes. Did I tell you? He's from a very prominent family in Connecticut. Bankers. The Chamberlains—you must have heard of them. Yet here he is, in Brazil. I wonder why he isn't in the family business. He's very reticent and never talks about his family and of course one doesn't ask that kind of qeustion, but I sometimes wonder.'

Yet, despite the irritation of his unwelcome attentions, the next few weeks went by quickly. Chantal spent her mornings working out at the hotel health club, swimming in the ocean and playing the piano in the deserted bar. Usually she had lunch with her mother or Dominique, or both. They took her shopping for clothes in the afternoon, or to have her body worked over in various ways—herbal baths, steam baths, massages, facials, manicures, pedicures. Most of these procedures were gone through at the hotel. In the evening there was a steady diet of outings—dinners, theatre, parties.

For a while all this was fun and relaxing, but after a few weeks she began to feel restless.

She inspected her reflection in the mirror and had to admit she looked good. She had a healthy tan, her hair was glossy, her body trim and well curved, her skin smooth.

She was getting sick and tired of all the primping. A little was good, a lot was boring. All this self-absorption was making her feeble-minded. What she needed was a job. Something to make her think before her brains turned to mush.

A job. But first she needed to learn Portuguese, which should not be the biggest challenge of her life. Speaking

French fluently and Spanish fairly well as she did, Portuguese should come easily.

Uncle Matteus suggested a tutor and she began to study Portuguese—one hour a day, two hours a day. She played the piano longer and longer. She refused to go shopping for more clothes, telling her sister she had enough to last her a lifetime. Her cupboards were full of casual day-wear as well as silks and satins in a delicious array of colours—a racy mini dress by Yves Saint Laurent, a strapless satin by Valentino, a long, romantic creation of champagne-coloured lace. She owned a parade of Italian shoes to match the clothes. She loved dressing up, to look and feel beautiful, but enough was enough.

Instead of eating at the hotel she explored the surrounding area and had lunch at small pavement cafés and restaurants, giving her the opportunity to practise her Portuguese.

One Saturday, a month after arrival, she walked to her favourite restaurant to have some lunch. She sat at a small table on the shaded terrace, sipping a glass of *Guarana*, and watched the people—sunbathers crossing the road to the beach, ice-cream vendors, skinny shoe-shine boys with old faces and wary eyes. The tall, dark figure of Enrico Chamberlain in his immaculate three-piece black suit stood out against the brightness of the sunfilled day, stark and powerful. He stopped at her table.

'Slumming?' he enquired.

'Having lunch,' she said, pretending not to understand. She took one of the tiny speckled eggs from a dish on the table and began to peel it.

'I hope it will be up to your standards.'

'What is your idea of my standards, if I may ask? She kept he voice carefully even, but his presumptuous attitude infuriated her.

'The Palácio. Maxim's in Paris.'

'Maxim's is overrated,' she said with a nonchalant wave of her hand. She forced her face into an expression of world-weary boredom, which cost her some effort. Narrowing slightly, his eyes darkened with suspicion, which surprised her. Maybe he had sensed her mockery, she wasn't sure. She wished he would move on and leave her alone. In the hotel she ran into him constantly, or so it seemed. Now she had left the hotel and she still ran into him, or rather he ran into her. 'Are you following me around?'

'Following you?' One dark brow rose in question. 'Certainly not.' He took a chair and joined her. 'I came out to have some lunch.'

'Slumming?'

His mouth quirked. 'Of course. I want my Saturday fix of *feijoado*—rice and beans. Brazilian poor man's food. Care to join me?'

'Why do you come here? Why not have your lunch at the hotel?'

'I need a change of scene,' he said calmly, taking a large black olive from the dish in the middle of the table. 'If I'm not too busy, I like to get out for a walk and have lunch in one of the little places around here.' He waved at a waiter and the man, his black suit one size too small and stretched tight across his back and chest, rushed over to their table.

'Would you like another drink?' Enrico glanced at the empty bottle on the table. '*Guarana*—do you like it?'

'Yes.' She had been trying to figure out what it tasted like. A cross between Seven-up and apple juice, she had decided, a little fruitier, maybe. 'I'll have another one.'

'Maybe you should try *batida*, to be authentic. It's *cachaça* with lemon juice.'

'What's *cachaça*?'

'Fermented cane alcohol. Pretty foul stuff, but not bad mixed with lemon juice.'

'Sounds awful, but I'll try anything once.'

She let him order the lunch, *feijoado completa*, and wondered how she was going to manage to sit here and talk to him for the next hour or so. This man, so cool, so controlled, was a mystery. She wondered what hid behind the mask, behind the impeccable manner, those wintry eyes. Clearly, it was a mask. She had seen the heat of anger in his face, if only for a moment, and heard the cool voice explode. If he could be roused to anger, maybe he was capable of other emotions as well.'

She wondered what he thought of her, because, clearly, he thought something of her or she wouldn't feel those strange undercurrents. Indifference didn't produce those sarcastic tones in his voice, carefully masked as they might be.

He made her feel defensive. Behind the cool gaze he was carefully dissecting her, and finding her lacking. It was not a feeling that was unfamiliar to her. All her life she had felt that way in Illinois, where she had always been found wanting by her peers.

But this man across from her, long slender fingers spreading fish pâté on a cracker, did not even know her. What was it about her that he objected to? Or was she making too much of it?

She leaned her elbows on the table and looked right into his face. 'Why do you dislike me so?'

Dark eyebrows rose. 'Dislike you? I don't even know you.'

'Exactly. You don't know me, and you quite dislike me. From the moment I set foot in the hotel, to be exact.'

He looked at her coolly. 'You're imagining things, Ms Stevenson.'

She felt like hitting him. 'No, I am not. You've been very polite and very hostile and cold enough to freeze a penguin. Don't you want me in your hotel? Do I embarrass you? Do I not fit in with you blue-blooded, wealthy guests?'

The mockery was ill-concealed. 'You fit in perfectly, Ms Stevenson—wealthy and elegant and full of French breeding.'

She gave a short laugh. 'Whatever gave you that idea? Matteus's wife is my mother, but I'm a country doctor's daughter. I grew up in a place called Perrydale, Illinois. Just ordinary folks out there, I assure you.'

The scepticism in his eyes was hard to miss.

'Don't you believe me?'

'I was under the impression that your father was a prominent physician in a prestigious research hospital in Chicago.'

She stared at him. 'You've got to be kidding. Whoever told you that?' Sudden anger surged through her and she held up her hand. 'Never mind, I can guess who told you that.' Dominique, of course. What was the matter with her, telling lies like that?

'I hear you are studying Portuguese,' said Enrico.

'I am.'

'Are you planning to settle in Brazil?'

She shrugged. 'I really don't know what I want to do. I'm . . . I'm at a loose end at the moment.'

'Loose end . . . very unsettling, I presume.'

She felt her body tense. 'You've never been at a loose end?'

One corner of his mouth moved up. 'No, never.'

'I imagine you always knew exactly what you wanted.'

He took a roll from the basket and broke it in two. 'Yes. Ever since I was fourteen or fifteen.'

'At that age you knew you wanted to manage a hotel? Is your father in the hotel business?' Dumb question, she thought. His father was a banker, probably, like the rest of his family. That's what her mother had just told her.

He spread butter on his roll. 'My father is dead. And no, he was not in the hotel business.' His tone was curt and it was obvious that he did not intend to discuss his father.

The food arrived on a large platter and the waiter ceremoniously filled their plates with the rice, beans, meat and several orange slices. The soupy black beans did not look particularly appetising and the blackish colour of the meat indicated it had been cooked along with the beans.

'What kind of meat is that?' she asked after the waiter retreated.

'Beef and pork.' His eyes challenged her. 'Smoked ox tongue, to be exact, and spare ribs, and the beans are cooked up with bacon and a pig's trotter as well.'

If he was expecting her to give some reaction of disgust, he had a long wait coming. She picked up her knife and fork. 'Sounds good,' she said lightly, and proceeded to take a bite of the beans.

And it was good. The beans had a delicious smoky flavour, as did the meat, and she ate with appetite. She wondered if Enrico was surprised, but there was not way of telling—his face showed no emotion.

They finished the meal with *cafezinhos*, tiny cups of very strong black coffee, skipping dessert for lack of room. He paid for the meal, refusing arrogantly to let her pay for her own food. It made her furious, but she kept her cool.

They walked back to the hotel in silence and the uniformed doorman greeted both of them as if they were royalty. The rush of water from the fountain filled the lobby with peaceful, soothing sounds, and as they

approached it she noticed Dominique and little Nicole.
Nicole was hanging over the marble edge trying to climb in,
and Dominique grabbed her and swung her back to the
floor. The child wailed in disappointment, complaining in a
torrent of heated French that her mother never allowed her
to do anything. She stopped in mid-sentence as she saw
Chantal and her face lit up. She rushed forward and flung
herself into Chantal's arms.

Chantal hugged the small body to her, smiling at the
enthusiasm of her three-year-old niece. She stopped smiling
as she noticed Dominique's face. It had again that oddly
frozen look about it, tight and expressionless. Her voice was
frigidly polite as she returned Enrico's equally polite
greeting. A repeat performance of the time she, Chantal,
had arrived at the hotel and Enrico had greeted them.

It was suddenly quite clear why Dominique had not made
her appearance at the cocktail party the night of that same
day. Enrico. She didn't want to be where Enrico was.

Dominique extracted her daughter from Chantal's
embrace. 'We've got to go, *chérie*. *Grand-mère* is waiting for
us.' She lifted the struggling child in her arms and walked
off. 'I'll see you later,' she said to Chantal over her
shoulder.

'I'll check if there's any mail for me,' Chantal said to
Enrico, expecting him to go his way, which he didn't. He
fell into step with her as they crossed the lobby.

'If there is, they should deliver it to your room.'

'Oh, they do, but I'm down here now.'

The desk clerk say her approach. 'Ms Stevenson, we just
received a message for you over the telex.' He handed her a
piece of paper and glanced fearfully at Enrico who stood by
her side. 'It arrived only a minute ago.'

She unfolded the paper and felt a knot of unease lodge in

her chest. Another message from M in Minneapolis. 'I'M
NOT GOING TO LET YOU DO THIS TO ME. IF
YOU DON'T STOP NOW, YOU'LL BE SORRY.' She
stared at the words, rereading them again. She looked at her
name at the top of the paper, the hotel's telex number. This
was crazy! Who was sending her these messages? What was
this all about? *What* was she supposed to be doing to this
unknown person in Minneapolis while staying in a hotel in
Rio?

The paper trembled in her hand and she wadded it in a
ball and stuffed it in the pocket of her white shorts.

Enrico observed her, frowning. 'What's wrong?'

'Nothing.' She turned away and moved towards the bank
of lifts, gritting her teeth when she realised he was
following her. He put a hand on her shoulder as soon as the
were out of sight of the hotel clerks at the desk.

'Is this another telex from Minneapolis?'

'I don't believe this is any of your business.'

It probably wasn't an answer he often received because
she saw sudden sparks of fire in his eyes.

'Don't be so stubborn,' he ground out. 'I saw your face
when you read that paper. If there's a problem, I want to
know about it.'

'Why? Are you my big brother or something?'

He clenched his jaws together and for an endless moment
his eyes burned into hers. Then, without a word, he turned
on his heel and strode off.

Standing perfectly still, she watched him go.

What was the matter with him? Then she shrugged. She
didn't care, and if she needed help, she most certainly
wouldn't ask Enrico Chamberlain.

She took the lift up to her room and stood in front of the
window overlooking the sea, wondering what to do. She

took the paper out of her pocket, smoothed it out and reread it. She was aware of a growing sense of apprehension. She had more or less ignored the first telex, now she wasn't sure what to do. She didn't even know what it was all about, which was worst of all. She had racked her brain, thinking of people whose names began with M and hadn't come up with an plausible candidates. She turned away from the window, tossing the paper on the table. It was stupid to let it bother her. Minneapolis was thousand of miles away.

She sat down at the desk and took out her Portuguese books and tried to study, but couldn't concentrate. She was beginning to feel drowsy with the heavy meal of rice and beans in her stomach and she pushed the books aside and lay down on the bed. As soon as she drifted into sleep, the phone rang. With a groan she groped for the phone next to the bed.

'Hello?'

'Chantal? It's me. You sound funny.'

Dominique. Chantal yawned. 'I'm in bed. I was asleep.'

There was a barely perceptible pause. 'I want to talk to you.' Dominique sounded oddly uncertain. 'Are you alone?'

'Alone? Of course I'm alone.'

'I'm at *Maman's*. I'll be right over.'

'Can't it wait? I'm beat. I want to take a nap.'

'I'm not disturbing anything, am I?'

Chantal gave a short laugh. 'No, you are not. I'm on the bed with my clothes on and there's no man in here, if that's what you're worried about.'

'Well, I was wondering.'

'Good lord, Dominique! I've been here a month. Who would I be sleeping with?'

'Oh, various possibilities spring to mind, but then you

never were a fast mover.

Chantal sighed and rolled her eyes to the ceiling. 'What did you want to talk about?'

'I'll come over.'

'Oh, all right then.' She probably wouldn't go back to sleep now, anyway. She ordered coffee and splashed cold water on her face and put on some fresh lipstick. Dominique and the coffee arrived at the same time, eight minutes later.

Chantal poured each of them a cup and Dominique draped herself in a chair and smoothed her skirt with a perfectly manicured hand. She surveyed the room, scrutinising the furniture, the curtains, the wallpaper.

'Not bad, this place. How do you like it here?'

'It's lovely. Very comfortable and pleasant. I didn't know how tired and weary I was until I came here. I guess this is just what I needed. For a while, anyway.'

'I'm glad then that I managed to get you out here. After my divorce, Uncle Matteus said I could come back to live here if I wanted to, but I got attached to the apartment. After all the work getting it just the way I wanted it, I felt I should stay around to enjoy the results.' She sipped carefully from the small cup.

After they were married, Dominique and her husband had moved into a luxurious penthouse apartment that Dominique had overhauled completely in the months before the wedding, spending staggering amounts of money and wearing out a succession of decorators. After the divorce, she and the baby stayed in the apartment and her ex-husband moved elsewhere. Chantal had never quite understood what had caused the break-up; her sister had been locked in a bitter silence and had refused to discuss it. Dominique and baby Nicole had spent the first Christmas

after the divorce in Illinois, and Chantal remembered well
how all her efforts to draw out her sister had failed
miserably.

The coffee was hot and strong. Chantal stirred sugar into
it, and glanced at her sister.

'So, what did you want to talk about?'

Dominique frowned and straightened in her chair. 'I saw
you come into the lobby with Enrico.'

'Yes, so I did.'

'Where did you go with him?'

Chantel stared at her, and Dominique waved her hand
carelessly. 'OK, I know what you're going to say. It's none
of my business, but . . .'

'We had lunch together.'

Dominique sighed. 'Chantal, I know it's none of my
business what you do, but I'm going to tell you something
and I hope you'll listen to me.'

Chantal settled back in her chair. 'All right, tell me.'

'Don't get involved with Enrico Chamberlain.'

Chantal almost laughed. 'Why not?'

'He's a bastard. He's hard and cold and when he's done
with you he drops you cold.'

'Sounds charming. Do you speak from personal
experience?'

'No.' Dominique stared in her cup. 'We never had an
affair, if that's what you mean.'

'So what happened between you and him?'

'Nothing.' There was a strange glitter in the blue eyes.

She's lying, Chantal thought. She put her cup on the
table. 'Is he married, by any chance?'

Dominique gave a humourless little laugh. 'No. You're
safe on that score. I don't think he'll ever get married. He'll
never find anybody good enough for him.' Her tone was

caustic. She stood up restlessly. 'Please, Chantal, be careful with him. Promise me.'

'Maybe you should first tell me what happened between you. You don't fool me, Dominique.'

Her sister flushed, but it took only a moment before she had collected her cool.

'I told you—nothing.'

Chantal sighed. 'All right, Dominique, don't tell me. But I'm not stupid and I'm not blind. I know what happens when you see him. I know you didn't come to the cocktail party the night I arrived because he was there . . .'

'I had a headache.'

Dominique, those headaches of yours are pure fiction! she wanted to say, but kept silent. She didn't want an argument with her sister. She poured another cup of coffee and her eyes caught the telex on the table.

'Read this,' she said to Dominique, gesturing at the paper.

'What is it?'

'A telex from Minneapolis.'

Dominique picked up the paper and read it, frowning.

'*Mon Dieu*! What is this all about?'

'I haven't the foggiest idea. I don't know anybody in Mineapolis. I've about melted my brain thinking. There was another one, a few weeks ago. It makes no sense at all.'

'Could it be from David? What's his last name?'

'David Anthony Henredon. And he lives in Chicago. Really, Dominique, I've thought of everybody.'

Dominique frowned. 'Well, maybe it's just somebody's sick idea of a joke. It happens all the time.' Her voice lacked conviction.

Chantal took a swallow of her coffee. 'Well, there isn't much I can do, so I might as well not worry about it.'

The problem was, she couldn't help worrying about it.

CHAPTER THREE

EVERY time Chantal entered her suite, she looked fearfully at the coffee table and at the silver tray that held messages and mail. She was furious with herself for being so obsessed with the telexes, but she couldn't help herself. However, after a few days, she began to relax. Dominique was probably right; it had to be some nut with a weird sense of humour.

After one more week of lounging around on the beach and playing the piano for hours on end, Chantal had had enough. If she didn't find herself something useful to do she would go crazy. Uncle Matteus was in Madrid, acquiring a new hotel. He had been gone for a week and would stay away for a couple more. She didn't want to wait. She would ask Enrico. After all, he was the GM and he had told her to come to him any time she needed something. Well, she needed something now.

A secretary in silk and pearls guarded the inner office. She was blonde and gorgeous and haughty in the extreme. A princess, that one. She spoke British English with only the slightest of Portuguese accents and she gave Chantal a condescending smile as she opened the door for her into Enrico's inner sanctum. Chantal disliked her on sight.

Chantal smiled back. 'There's lipstick on your teeth,' she whispered, gratified to see the look of horror replace the arrogance on the beautiful face.

Enrico's office was sumptuous and imposing, sleek and contemporary apart from the massive antique desk that dominated the room. This sat in solitary splendour in the middle of the large room and behind it sat Enrico leafing through the pages of a folder in front of him. A king in his kingdom, immaculate in his elegant black suit and white silk shirt.

'Please have a seat,' he said, indicating a chair. 'I'll be with you in a moment.'

Chantal sat down and examined the oil paintings on the wall. Originals, and valuable ones, no doubt. The scenes intrigued her. One depicted an old woman sitting in front of a small village house, her wrinkled face weary and worried as if she no longer could cope with the burden of living. Another showed fishermen selling their meagre catch on the beach. A third pictured a few ragged children playing barefoot in the dirt, a large, silver-grey Mercedes gleaming in the background.

They were not at all the sort of paintings she would expect to find in Enrico's office. They formed an odd contrast to the man and to the wealthy surroundings.

'What do you think?'

She turned to face him. 'They're beautiful paintings.

He noddded. 'My secretary thinks I should throw them out and get something more appropriate. Something starkly modern, preferably.'

'I'm not surprised,' she said drily.

His mouth quirked. 'You don't agree with her?'

'No. I doubt there's much we'd agree on.'

The corner of his mouth tilted and she noticed a spark of humour in the grey eyes. 'Do I detect a note of . . . shall we say . . . dislike?'

'Yes, you could say that.'

'Have you met her before? Or is this a first-impression judgement?'

'The latter.'

'Interesting.' The smile was amused and it did wonders for the sharp severity of his features. He pushed the folder to one side. 'So, I understand you wanted to talk to me.'

'Yes.' She straightened in her chair. 'I would like you to help me find a job.'

Surprise briefly flashed in his eyes. 'Here, in the hotel?'

'Yes.'

'I see. And what are your talents?' His tone indicated he doubted she had any. Anger sang in her ears, but she was determined not to show it.

'Oh, I can make beds, wash dishes, vacuum floors, clean bathrooms.'

He cocked one eyebrow. 'Is that so?'

She nodded. 'I'm very good, actually. I can also type, use the computer, answer the telephone and make peanut butter sandwiches.

His mouth quirked. 'You must be the Cinderella of the family.'

'Hardly,' she said coolly. 'And what is wrong with making beds or typing? Honest work, isn't it?'

There was a moment's silence. 'Quite,' he said then, and she wondered if she had imagined the odd note in his voice. His eyes narrowed slightly as he scrutinised her.

'Why do you want to work? If I am not mistaken, you are a woman of independent means.'

'But not one of leisure. I'm not used to doing nothing indefinitely. I've always worked. I've been here almost six weeks now and I've enjoyed it tremendously. But now . . .' she shrugged, 'it's time to feel useful again, to do something. Besides, I don't want to sponge off my stepfather for the rest of my life.'

He gave a mocking little laugh. 'Your stepfather has more money than he knows what to do with. Believe me, you . . .'

'The vastness of his riches is beside the point. The issue here is my personal feelings. I have two hands and a good brain and

I'd like to use them. There are other things in life besides money, nice as that may be. There are the minor matters of responsibility, respect, a sense of self-worth.'

'Well, well, I'm impressed.'

Rage boiled inside her; she trembled with it. How dare he speak to her like this? She clenched her hands into fists, struggling for composure, swallowing to find her voice. 'I realise that you're too good for this world,' she said, her voice amazingly controlled, 'and that you have nothing but contempt for other people, but . . .'

He waved his hand in imperious dismissal. 'Don't over-react, please.'

His condescending manner was more than she could swallow, more than she was prepared to take from him or anyone else. Mustering all her self-control, she came to her feet, anchoring them to the floor to steady herself. She glared at him hard. 'Do you treat everyone this way, or is this just reserved for me? You are rude and offensive and you're demonstrating an appalling lack of professionalism, Mr General Manager.' She turned and crossed the room to the door.

'Wait!'

She kept right on going, opened the door, closed it calmly behind her and made her way through the outer office without even looking at the princess in pearls.

To hell with him.

She saw him again the next morning at the beach as she was coming out of the water after a bracing swim in the cold water. He was running along the water's edge, wearing only black swimming-trunks and white running shoes.

She pretended not to see him, but he stopped dead in front of her, breathing hard from exertion.

'*Bom dia.*'

She looked up. 'Good morning,' she said coolly, and walked past him to where her towel lay in the sand, hearing his footsteps behind her. She picked up the towel and began to dry herself.

'I'd like to talk with you,' Enrico said. He wiped the damp hair off his forehead and rested his hands on his hips. He had a broad chest with black, curly hair and his skin glistened with perspiration.

'I have absolutely nothing to say to you,' she said icily, rubbing her hair hard with the towel.

'I owe you an apology.'

'You've got to be kidding. The emperor never apologises, haven't you heard?'

The left corner of his mouth turned down. 'I suppose I had that coming.'

And a whole lot more, she wanted to say, but kept silent. He looked disturbingly virile standing there in the morning sunshine, his dark skin gleaming. His untidy hair gave him a slightly rakish look, less controlled and severe. It was difficult to accept that this man was the same as the cold, arrogant man in black. She found it unnerving to be in such close proximity to this vibrant, practically naked male. She was also uneasily aware of wearing nothing but a skimpy swimsuit. By Rio standards she was probably overdressed, since the most minuscule of bikinis appeared to be the norm, but she felt anything but overdressed.

She wrapped her towel around her sarong-style, slipped on her thongs and made for the hotel. All the way to the road, she felt his eyes on her, but he didn't follow.

Before crossing the road, she cast a quick glance behind her, noticing Enrico wading into the water, then diving into an oncoming wave.

'I said I owed you an apology.'

Enrico stood next to her table in the roof-top solarium where she was eating her breakfast, looming over her. He was dressed again in his infernal black suit, his hair neatly combed, smelling faintly of aftershave.

'What exactly are you aplogising for?' she asked.

'For being rude, insensitive and overbearing.'

She put her hand over her heart. 'You're going to give me heart failure.'

He raised his brow. 'It's that bad, is it?'

She nodded. 'Yes, it is that bad.'

He pulled out a chair and sat down, uninvited, and sighed. 'I have a terrible feeling that somewhere along the line I've made a mistake.'

'What kind of mistake?'

'I'm not quite sure, but I'll work on it. Do you mind if I join you for breakfast?'

'I'm almost done. You can have the table to yourself.'

'Keep me company. Have another cup of coffee.'

As if on cue, a waiter materialised with his two pots, one with coffee, the other with hot milk, and poured each of them a cup.

Enrico came to his feet and gestured at the lavish spread in the buffet tables. 'Let me get some food. Don't go away.' He smiled. 'Please.'

She was sorely tempted, but it was the smile and the 'please' that made her stay. He confused her, and it was disturbing. He was beginning to show signs of being human.

He brought back two big plates of food and set out to eat with appetite.

'You're going to eat all that?' she asked, amazed.

'I'm hungry,' he said reasonably. 'It's eight-thirty and I've been up since five.'

'You always get up so early?'

'Usually. I work for an hour or two, then go running or swimming, then have breakfast and after that go back to work.' He buttered a bread roll and topped it with ham and cheese. 'I like doing paperwork early in the morning. No interruptions, no telephone. I can really work myself through a pile of paper.'

She drank her coffee and watched him eat. He consumed every single thing on his two plates, then asked for more coffee.

'So,' he said, 'what did you do for a living before you came here?'

'I managed a small country inn in Perrydale, Illinois.'

Surprise flashed across his features. 'Ah, a colleague.'

'Hardly. We had twenty-four rooms and a restaurant.'

He leaned back in his chair. 'Tell me about it.'

She wondered why he was interested. She shrugged lightly. 'You know the kind of place I'm talking about. Basic accommodation, friendly atmosphere, simple, home-cooked food.' She smiled. 'All the rooms look different. The floors and stairs creak. The bathrooms are old and small and some even have bathtubs with claw feet.'

He nodded. 'What about you?'

'What about me? I managed it.'

He studied her for a moment. 'When you asked me for a job, you were not seriously intending to make beds and clean bathrooms, were you?'

'Given any choice, no. I'm not that crazy about housework in general, but it isn't beneath me, if that's what you think. As a matter of fact, working with other women might be a good way to perfect my Portuguese. For a while, anyway.' She took a sip of her coffee and looked at him blandly. 'From there on I could work my way up, learn the business from the inside out.' She leaned her elbows on the table and smiled sweetly. 'Then

I'd become the General Manager.'

He laughed, he actually laughed. At least he did have a sense of humour. It was a comfort of sorts. Then his face returned to its normal cool expression and he frowned.

'You're quite serious about wanting a job at the Palácio?'

'Yes.'

'Have you discussed this with Matteus?'

'No.'

His frown deepened. 'I didn't think so. I doubt very much whether he'll agree to your doing any sort of work here at the Palácio.'

'Why not?'

'Appearances. It wouldn't look right—his stepdaughter working in his hotel. Cinderella, and all that.'

'I don't care what it looks like!'

'But he does,' he said calmly. 'And I'm afraid he's the boss.'

A few days later she received a phone-call from her grandfather. He had called her several times before, asking how she was.

'How are you doing?' he asked, his voice gruff. She knew his concern was real; the more worried he was the more gruff his voice.

'I'm all right, *Grand-père*, really.'

'Well, you rest, you hear? You take all the time you need. Catch some sun, put some flesh on those bones. Your mother was telling me you're too thin.'

Chantal laughed. 'It won't last. The food at the Palácio is very good, and they're all spoiling me.'

'You deserve it, child. You've had a rough time.'

'I'm getting better. Don't worry.'

'There's something I want you to think about.' He cleared his throat, which was an indication that the matter at hand was an important one. 'I want you to come to Paris and join the company.'

'Join the company?' She wasn't sure she had heard right.

'Don't play dumb. You know what I mean. I've mentioned it before.'

'I thought you were joking.' Her grandfather was eighty and his ideas about a woman's place in society belonged in the Stone Age.

'I never joke.'

This was not true, but she did not argue with him. 'You've got Uncle Albert, and Bertrand and Jean-Jacques.' Her French uncle and two cousins were perfectly capable of running the company. Her grandfather had always considered the women in his family to be merely decorative objects—beloved and cherished, but not particularly useful when it came to business. Chantal had had good-natured arguments with him about this, but she had no intentions, or hopes, or changing the mind of an eighty-year-old patriarch who had ruled the family businesses with an iron hand for almost six decades without the help of females.

'We need all the help we can get, and I'm not getting any younger. It's time you came in and learned to do your share.'

She grinned into the phone. 'Is this just a ploy to get me to come to France?' She couldn't believe that he was serious. 'Are you going to make me answer the phone and open the mail? I'm too smart to fall for that, *Grand-père*.'

'I should hope so!' he growled. 'Think about it!' Then, without a goodbye, he hung up.

Chantal grinned as she replaced the receiver. Her grandfather never was one to waste his time with niceties.

It was very dark in the bar, but she liked it that way. Outside the sun gloried over the city and the beaches, but here all was cool and dark with only the piano lamp throwing its light over the music and the keys. Here she had her own little world protected by the dark around her.

She played the piano for over two hours, the music transporting her to some magical place full of feeling and beauty and peace. She finished with one of her favourite Chopin sonatas, then sat still for a few moments, hands at rest on the keys, eyes closed. It was difficult, sometimes, to stop, to work herself out of the trance-like state the music created in her.

'Ah, such elegance, such emotion.'

Startled, she turned around to find Enrico standing behind her, looking down at her with a faint smile.

'Chopin, wasn't it?'

She nodded. 'Yes.' She had not heard him coming. She had not known he had been there, listening to her music. It was a strangely disturbing thought. Her playing here in the bar was a personal thing, something she did for herself, not for others.

'You play beautifully.' No mockery now in the voice.

'Thank you,' she said quietly.

'I didn't know you played the piano. We can have one put in your room, if you like.'

'No, no. As long as no one minds me using this one.'

'I've heard no complaints.' He smiled. 'And I certainly don't expect any.'

There was a silence. She felt awkward just sitting there with Enrico towering over her, but she wasn't sure what to do. Get up and walk away? Slowly she came to her feet, lowered the lid and gathered her music. Then she switched off the light and everything was suddenly very dark around them.

'You have a real gift,' he said softly. 'Do you realise that?'

'I enjoy playing. It has always been . . . important to me to play.'

'Important?'

'As a way to clear my mind, to get in tune with myself.'

'Like yoga, or meditating.'

'Yes, I suppose so.'

In the darkened room they faced each other in silence. She had the strangest feeling that something was happening, but she had no idea what.

'Are you free for dinner tonight?' he asked at last.

'I'm having dinner with my mother and some of her friends.'

'Can you get out of it?'

'Yes, I suppose so.'

'Good. I'll come for you at eight.' He turned and strode off and she watched him go, clutching the music against her chest. She stood in the shadowed room for a long moment, wondering why he had asked her and why she had accepted.

CHAPTER FOUR

'I HAVE a confession to make.'

Chantal smiled faintly. Enrico had a confession to make? Amazing. 'I'm shocked,' she said, mildly mocking.

She sat across from him at a table in a small, intimate restaurant with a cosy, homely abience. Candles on the table, white cotton table cloth, pink carnations, soft piano music in the background. Not the exclusive, sophisticated place she had expected from a polished, cosmopolitan type like Enrico. A strange man. A man of contrasts. She thought of the large Victorian desk in his sleek, modern office. She remembered his voice, quiet, sincere: *You play beautifully.*

She had taken a long time to get dressed, feeling nervous and uncertain, and angry at herself for feeling that way. Why had she accepted the invitation? Because it was unexpected? Dangerous? Because it was, in some strange way, a challenge? She must be out of her mind.

She stood in front of her cupboard wondering what to wear, her eyes sliding over the beautiful clothes—the silks and taffetas and lace, the lovely colours. She could wear something clingy and extravagant, but for some reason it didn't seem like a good idea. She opted for something simple and elegant in creamy yellow that showed off her tan nicely. Silky tights and high-heeled sandals completed the outfit. She brushed her long hair back to one side and held it in place with a comb.

Dominique knocked on her door as she was almost ready. She swept into the room in a daring creation of violet silk and black lace. Strapless and ankle-length, the dress was stunning.

'You look gorgeous,' Chantal said.

'Thanks. I came up to see if you wanted to come to a party with me after we've had dinner with *Maman*.'

'I cancelled dinner with *Maman*. I'm going out.'

'Oh, I didn't know.'

'It came up unexpectedly. Bu thanks for the invitation.' Chantal stood in front of the mirror and smoothed her hair. Dominique watched her, saying nothing, obviously expecting more information.

'Where are you going?' she asked at last.

Chantal met her eyes in the mirror. 'I'm going out to dinner with Enrico.'

Dominique stiffened. 'I warned you not to get involved with him.'

'Having dinner does not constitute "getting involved with", Dominique. And I'm not sure I understood your reasons for warning me.'

'He's a bastard!' she said hotly. 'I'm trying to save you from yourself, don't you understand that?'

'I'll be careful.'

Dominique stared at her hard, then turned on her heel, opened the door and swung out of the room. Chantal sighed. Dominique was holding out. She wondered what it was that her sister refused to tell her.

Enrico knocked on her door at exactly eight. He looked tall and elegant and as imposing as ever, but the black suit was gone. Instead he wore a stylish pale grey suit of a more casual cut and no tie. She was annoyed by the nervous flutter in her stomach. So the man was handsome; she had known plenty of handsome men.

'I thought women were always late,' he commented, apparently surprised to find her ready to go.

'Not me. Barring house fires, floods and earthquakes, I'm

always ready. It probably signifies great unresolved fears and insecurities,' she said lightly, 'at least according to an amateur Freud I once knew.'

'What kinds of fears?' He closed the door behind her and they walked to the elevator.

'Abandonment, missing the train, losing out on the fun, who knows?'

He pushed the lift button. 'You don't seem the insecure type to me.'

You wouldn't say that if you knew how I felt, she thought, trying to relax. This was ridiculous. The lift doors opened, saving her from a reply. She wondered how she was going to make it through the evening with him.

And now he was sitting across the table from her telling he had a confession to make, which seemed quite out of character.

'Why are you shocked?' he asked.

'You don't seem the type to confess to anything, ever.'

He smiled. 'Only to minor sins. I've been listening to your piano playing for the past week. This morning was not the first time.'

'Oh.' She frowned. 'I never noticed you.'

'I didn't want you to notice me. Where did you learn to play?'

'In Perrydale at first, and later in Chicago. I started when I was six.'

'Did you hate it? The discipline, the practice?'

'Hate it? No, of course not. I wanted to be the greatest piano player in the world, so I did what I was supposed to do.' She smiled. 'And here I am, *not* the greatest piano player in the world.'

'But a great one.'

'A good one.'

He shook his head. 'So much discipline, and modest too.'

His voice was lightly teasing, but held no mockery.

'I'm glad you find some redeeming qualities in me,' she said mildly.

'Why wouldn't I?'

'Because I didn't expect you to be looking for them, frankly. I've been wondering about all that disapproval you've been radiating.' She took a sip of her wine. 'Does it have anything to do with my sister, Dominique, by any chance.'

In the soft light his face went hard. She was not imagining it.

He shrugged, his features relaxing almost immediately. 'Why don't we leave your sister out of the conversation?'

'Why? Is there something I should know?'

'Maybe you should ask her.' He picked up the menu and glanced at the listings. 'Have you decided?' The subject of Dominique was closed.

They ordered the food and nibbled away at the olives, the tiny quail eggs, and the bread and pâté already on the table. They talked about the Palácio. He asked her about the inn in Perrydale and about leaving her job there before coming to Brazil.

'I was ready to quit, anyway,' she said. 'I didn't like what the owner wanted to do. The Perrydale Inn has charcter, and he wanted to ruin it all—standardise the rooms, modernise the bathrooms, make it into some featureless motel. I couldn't stand the idea.'

'Will you ever go back to Perrydale again?'

'To live? No. I have no other family there. My father was an only child and his parents died several years ago. They had him late in life.'

'You lived there all your life and you have no ties there now? What about friends?'

'I had two close friends in school. Both moved away after college.' She played with her fork. 'I never did feel I belonged there. I wish I had. Perrydale is a nice, friendly place.'

'Were you more at home in France?'

She gave an uncertain little shrug. 'I went to Cap d'Antibes every summer to be with my mother and the rest of my French family. I loved it there, but still, it wasn't home.' She frowned. 'It was strange. I never knew where I belonged. In the States I felt French and in France I felt American.

He nodded. 'I know what you mean.'

She took a sip of her wine. 'I always felt pulled between two worlds. I loved going to France in the summer, but I missed my father.

In Illinois she missed her French family and the bright, glittery life, the parties, the careless joy of a lazy summer, the wonderful food, the interesting people.

She felt like two people leading two different lives.

'What do you consider you home?' she asked. 'Brazil? The States?'

He lifted his hand in a careless gesture. 'Neither, I suppose. When I was young I felt very American. I *was* American.'

'You have family in the States, right?'

'Technically, yes.' The bitterness in his voice did not escape her, although she was aware that he had attempted to sound cool and emotionless.

'What about your family here? Do they live in Rio?'

'No. Up north, in Bahia. My mother and younger sister, and a slew of aunts, uncles and cousins. My other sister lives in São Paulo. She's married and has two kids.' He smiled vaguely. 'Two boys. Hellions.'

'How long did you live in the States?'

'I lived in Connecticut until I was fifteen. My father died when I was thirteen. Two years later we moved to Brazil, to live with my mother's family.'

'It must have been quite a change in your life.'

'Yes. I spoke Portuguese, but I wasn't truly a Brazilian. I felt like a foreigner here.'

The food arrived. *'Bom apetite,'* Enrico said, after the waiter had served them. For a while they concentrated on eating. The food was delicious, an interesting concoction of seafood, rice and vegetables.

She asked him about the Geneva hotel he had managed and for a while they talked about Europe—Switzerland, England, about her summers in France.

'You didn't want to live with your mother permanently?'

'I wanted to live with both my father and mother,' she said wryly. 'But I had to make a choice. I chose my father.'

'Why?'

She hesitated. 'He was a very special man. I loved him.' She swallowed at the constriction in her throat. 'Everybody loved him. He was more than just a doctor to the people in Perrydale. He cared about them and their problems.' She bit her lip and looked down on her plate. It was still hard to talk about her father without getting emotional.

'And your mother? How did you feel about her?'

She kept her eyes fixed on her plate, feeling her face grow warm. Her feelings for her mother had been so mixed up during her younger years. For a while she had hated her for breaking up the family, but it hadn't lasted. She had eventually made her peace, had learned a certain measure of understanding and forgiveness.

'I'm sorry,' he said quietly. 'I have no right to ask you that.'

'As a child I admired my mother,' she said softly. 'I was in awe of her. To me she was the most beautiful woman in the world.' With her elegant French designer clothes, her softly curling dark hair and beautiful jewellery, she didn't belong in Perrydale. French and chic, her mother was different from all the other mothers, who wore jeans and baked apple pies. Her nails were always polished, her face always made up, her hair always right. Her cooking was abominable.

Her father was the one who read her stories and held her on his lap when she had hurt herself, the one who woke at night to comfort her when she had had a bad dream. Her father always listened. Her mother always talked.

Until the divorce her life had been perfect. She had been proud of her doctor father, proud of her beautiful mother. Afterwards her feelings had become so difficult and painful.

'Why did your parents get a divorce?'

It was a rather intimate question, but it didn't seem to matter now. She seldom talked about her family, but for some strange reason, it did not seem so difficult now in the subdued lighting of the restaurant. Carefully she brushed a bread crumb off the table. 'My mother didn't belong in Perrydale. She tried for eleven years and never adjusted.'

Her parents had loved each other, but love had not been enough to sustain her mother's thirst for a more stimulating life than Perrydale had to offer. As a country doctor with an overload of patients, her husband could not give her more than an occasional evening out in Chicago, and an early vacation in the South of France. It wasn't enough. Not until much later did Chantal realise how terribly lonely her mother had been in the Perrydale years.'

Her father had been devastated by the divorce and had withdrawn into his work. He had never remarried, but always grieved for the marriage that didn't work, the wife he could not make happy.

Chantal looked up, finding Enrico studying her intently. His eyes saw too much and it made her uneasy. She wasn't sure she wanted him to guess all those secret, painful feelings. She wiped her mouth with her napkin and took a sip of her wine. 'What about your mother?' she asked. 'Did she like living in the States?'

A shuttered look came into his face. 'In the beginning, before my father died, yes. She missed her family, of course, but she seemed happy enough. She had a husband and three children, a big house, her own car, plenty of friends.

'Then why did she go back to Brazil?'

His mouth twisted bitterly. 'My father neglected to provide for his family. After his death there was . . . nothing.'

'Nothing?' She stared at him, surprised. 'I thought your family . . .' She stopped. 'I'm sorry.' From the look on his face it was obvious he didn't want to discuss the matter any further. She held out her glass. 'Is there more wine?'

The Chamberlains were a wealthy New England family of bankers. Old money, impeccable reputation. But Enrico's father had left his wife and children destitute. How was this possible? Was this what had made Enrico so cold and bitter? Or were there other reasons? It wasn't hard to guess why there was no close bond between Enrico and his American family.

Still, none of this had anything to do with her, and she still had found no answer to the question of why he had treated her so contemptuously when she had first arrived at the Palácio.

She became suddenly aware of the music. It had been in the background, hovering on the edge of her consciousness—pleasant, non-intruding. For a moment she stopped eating and listened. The pianist was playing Christmas carols. That very morning she had noticed in the hotel lobby the gigantic Christmas tree, a live specimen decorated with silver and crystal ornaments. It was one of the most beautiful trees she had ever seen, delicate and serene and sparkling.

'It seems strange to have Christmas in the summer,' she said. 'It's like some weird time-warp to be on the beach in the sun and then walk into the hotel and see that huge tree and hear the music. It's like the wires in my brain got crossed or something.'

'It was hard for me to get used to as well.'

She thought of all the Christmases she had spent with her father and Dominique, the warmth and excitement, the joy of seeing her sister again for a short while.

She gave a half-smile. 'You know what I miss? I miss having a kitchen.'

He frowned. 'A kitchen?'

'To do some Christmas baking. Cranberry nut bread, pumpkin pie, that sort of thing. I always enjoyed getting ready for the holidays, for Dominique's visit. She always spent Christmas in Illinois with my father and me.'

'You'll miss your father this Christmas,' he said quietly—a statement, not a question.

She nodded, surprised a little at his sensitivity. 'Yes.' Their eyes met and he gave her an odd, almost gentle little smile.

The waiter came to take their plates away. They ordered dessert, a simple but delicious mango sorbet with whipped cream. They ate it slowly, then lingered over their coffee, stretching the meal as if by unspoken consent.

The chuaffered car that had taken them to the restaurant took them back to the Palácio. It slid noiselessly through the lighted city streets. Neon lights flickered on and off. Christmas decorations brightened the shop windows. The streets were alive with people going to theatres or nightclubs or restaurants.

He took her straight to her suite, not suggesting another drink, and he took the keys from her and opened the door.

'Thank you,' she said, stepping inside. 'I enjoyed it.' It was even true, strangely enough.

He smiled. 'It was my pleasure.' He sounded rather formal, suddenly, and she smiled back at him. For a moment their eyes locked and she felt a thrill of something dangerous and exciting course through her. In the silvery depths of his eyes

she read an answering emotion, or was she imagining it?
Quickly she lowered her gaze, feeling her heart make a
ridiculous somersault in her chest.

'Goodnight, Enrico.'

'*Boa noite.*' He turned and was gone.

She closed the door and leaned against it with a sigh. She
wondered if he had expected her to invite him in, but wasn't
sure. One thing she couldn't fault him on was his behaviour.
The perfect gentleman, all right—no seductive gestures, no
veiled invitations, no goodnight kiss. She grimaced and then
laughed, an odd sound in the quiet room. She hadn't come
across many men like that lately.

Maybe Enrico Chamberlain was not capable of warm
emotions or romantic passion. Maybe women left him cold.

But somehow she doubted it. There was too much energy
between them, too much tension she couldn't explain.

Little Nicole was a delight, Chantal thought, as she watched
her little niece play at the water's edge. Wearing only tiny red
bikini panties, her sturdy little body was brown from her toes
to her hair-line. She was full of life and exuberant joy, her big
brown eyes shining with mischief. Everything was an
adventure. She danced and laughed and talked the entire time,
or so it seemed. She was being spoiled rotten by everybody—
her mother, her grandmother, Uncle Matteus, whom she
called *Grand-père,* yet so far Chantal had noticed few negative
effects of all the indulgence. She was a lovely child, a dark-
haired angel, her sister's little girl. But the child's father had
been disappointed she wasn't a boy and never even came to see
her.

Chantal pushed her sunglasses higher on her nose. It was
after four and the afternoon heat was beginning to fade. How
was it possible that a father was not interested in his own

child? What had happened between Sergio and Dominique?

Nicole was playing with an empty suntan lotion bottle, filling it with water and runing it out over her head, squeezing her eyes shut tight and squealing as the water dripped down her face and back. It was a joy to watch her and Chantal had not at all minded when Dominique had asked her to babysit Nicole for a couple of hours, and had listened patiently to a lengthy list of instructions.

Yes, she had promised, she would put sun block on the delicate little nose. She would make sure Nicole did not drown or step on a piece of glass or burn her feet on the hot sand or eat more than one ice-cream or talk to strangers or cross the street without holding hands.

'So, you're playing nanny today?'

Chantal looked up to find Enrico standing beside her, wearing blue shorts and an unbuttoned shirt. A red towel lay draped over one shoulder.

'Hi, I didn't see you. And yes, I'm babysitting.'

He sat down next to her in the sand and looked at Nicole who was digging a hole in the wet sand and filling it up with water from the bottle.

'Are you stopping work early today?' Chantal asked.

He sighed. 'I wish. No, I'll be working tonight and I needed a break, so here I am. A quick swim and back to the salt mines.'

'Do you often work such long days?'

'Seldom, actually, but I used to. Practically worked myself into the ground a few years ago.'

'Why?'

He shrugged. 'I had a lot of ambition but not a lot of good sense. I was eating, sleeping and breathing my work. I was always exhausted and had no time for a social life.'

'Doesn't sound like a lot of fun.'

He grimaced. 'No, it wasn't. I ended up with some stress-related health problems and I knew I'd better do something. I learned that in the long run I was more efficient and more productive if I paced myself and worked a normal day. I learned to leave my work at the office and not bring it home with me.'

'Was that in Switzerland?'

'Yes.' He jumped to his feet. 'Well, I'm going for a swim.' He took off his shirt and shorts, revealing black swimming-trunks. 'Mind if I leave these here?' he asked, dropping his things next to her towel. Without waiting for an answer, he strode towards the water, then stopped and said something in French to Nicole, who looked at him wide-eyed. He picked up the yellow plastic bottle and tossed it into the water. Nicole came to her feet and stood next to him watching the bottle bob up on a wave and spill back on to the sand a few feet away. She ran to get it, then ran back and gave it to Enrico.

'*Encore! Encore!*' she shouted, and once more Enrico took the bottle and threw it into the sea. Fascinated, Nicole watched as the bottle washed ashore again. 'It's magic!' she called. 'Magic! Magic!' She retrieved the bottle and rushed back to Enrico.

'*Encore, s'il vous plaît!*'

This went on for a number of times, and Chantal watched the two of them laughing and talking. Enrico's face was smiling and relaxed as he talked to the little girl, apparently quite at ease with a three-year-old. Again she was struck by the strange dichotomy of Enrico's character.

Finally, Enrico told Nicole to try it herself and went for his swim.

Who was this man? she wondered. Why was it that he was beginning to fascinate her? Obsess her like some puzzle that didn't want to be solved? In the last couple of days she had been thinking about him far too much, yet she couldn't help it. Every time she met him she was presented with another piece to the puzzle, a piece that seemed not to fit anything she already had.

It bothered her. It kept her busy. Words and phrases kept repeating themselves in her mind—things he had said, things her mother had mentioned, Dominique's warning.

Nicole had made herself wet all over and was now rolling around in the sand to see how much of it would stick. Apparently she had given up on the bottle.

Chantal looked out over the water to see if she could see Enrico, but in the distance she could not distinguish him from the several other swimmers.

I didn't have any kind of social life, he had said. She could easily see that a man like Enrico was a compulsive worker, or at least could have been if he no longer was now. She wondered about the women in his life, about the type of woman he found attractive. Was he as cold and distant in his personal relationships as he was in his capacity as GM?'

She was beginning to suspect he was not. He certainly seemed to have thawed considerably during their dinner together, and with Nicole he was friendly and amusing.

She watched him as he came back out of the water, feeling a restless uneasiness at the sight of his wet, brown body moving so easily across the sand. Without the sober suit, it was much easier to think of him as a warm-blooded, alive, breathing male. A man to touch. A man to kiss.

The thoughts came unbidden and she felt suddenly frightened by them. What am I thinking! she thought.

You're thinking what every normal healthy female would think under the circumstances, a little voice reassured her.

He reached for his towel and began to dry himself, dripping water on her leg. 'Well, that felt good,' he commented with a grin, rubbing his chest. She tried not to look at his chest. She tried not to look at him at all. He was too close and all her senses were wide awake. She was acutely aware of him, and of her own body in the skimpy swimsuit.

Nicole came running up. 'Do you have my bottle?' she asked Enrico.

'I gave it to you.'

'I threw it to you in the sea. I threw it far far far, so you could catch it.'

He looked at her regretfully. 'I didn't see it. I'm not a very good catcher.'

'I think a fish ate it. A shark. Did you see a shark out there?'

He shook his head. *'Non.'*

Nicole's eyes gleamed. 'Well, he was probably hiding 'cause he didn't want you to see him catch my bottle.'

Enrico nodded solemnly. 'You're probably right.'

Nicole began to giggle. 'He's gonna have a tummy ache!' She danced away, back to the water's edge.

Enrico grinned at Chantal. 'She's got a good imagination,' he said in English.

'She's a great kid.'

He nodded thoughtfully. 'Yes.'

She eyed him for a moment. 'Do you like children?'

'Sure. I get a kick out of them. I like to figure out what makes them tick. I'm eternally amazed how smart they are, and how often parents don't seem to realise they're being outwitted.'

'The voice of experience,' she said, mildly mocking. 'Wait till you have your own, then it will all seem different. The brightest people become pushovers for their own children.'

'How do you know that?'

She grinned. 'My father told me.'

Amusement shone in his eyes. 'Ah, of course.' He sat down

on his towel. 'So, Ms Stevenson, how many children do you want when you grow up?'

'Ten,' she said promptly. 'But then again, maybe only one.'

'Sounds reasonable,' he said gravely.

'What about you?'

'Me?' He squinted up at the sky, watching a blue and orange kite with a long green tail swooping through the air. 'I haven't decided yet.' He looked back at her and smiled. 'Who knows,' he added casually, 'maybe ten, maybe one.'

She looked into the grey eyes and suddenly her throat went dry. It was ridiculous to read anything into this. He hadn't meant anything with it. Yet somehow the words had taken on another meaning, were coloured with other possibilities. She saw the smile fade from his eyes and she looked away, glancing over at Nicole playing in the sand. She came to her feet and shook her hair behind her shoulders.

'I'd better clean her up a little and get back to the hotel.' She plodded through the sand towards Nicole.

Enrico waited for them and together they walked back to the road. They wiped the sand of their feet and slapped on thongs. On a stone bench nearby, three young boys were watching them. One had a shoe-shine kit between his feet. Their clothes were torn and dirty, their eyes wary and tired. It was the faces that always bothered her—seven or eight-year-olds looking like old men with none of the careless joy of childhood in their expressions. It was disturbing.

Evening traffic had started, a long stream of cars without a break. They had to wait at the kerb for the light to change before crossing the road, and Nicole dutifully gave each of them a hand.

We look like a family, Chantal thought, and the idea seemed so ridiculous that for a moment she wondered if she was losing all sense of reality.

'*C'est vert!*' Nicole changed as the light changed. 'It's green! It's green!'

They crossed the road, Nicle skipping between them. They entered the hotel through a side entrance especially for beachgoers, dropped off their wet, sandy towels and found their way to a bank of lifts.

'How about a swim in the morning?' Enrico asked Chantal as he pushed the button.

'What time?'

'Seven-thirty? Is that too early?'

She shook her head. 'No. I'm usually up by six or so.'

The lift doors opened and they got in. Nicole wanted to push the buttons, so Enrico lifted her up and showed her which ones to hit. She wanted to push them all, which he deftly prevented her from doing by tickling her in the ribs and making her laugh.

'I'll see you in the morning, then,' he said to Chantal, when he got off one floor before hers.

She nodded. 'I'll be there.'

It seemed to happen without plan. Every morning they met at the beach and went swimming together, then had breakfast at the solarium on the roof. It was a very relaxing routine, and to her amazement, Chantal was beginning to enjoy his company.

'I have a favour to ask,' he said one morning.

She looked at him suspiciously and he laughed. 'Boy, your trust in me is encouraging.'

'What is it?'

'My sister is coming to stay here for a week. I invited her here last year and she really enjoyed it. I wonder if you would spend some time with her.'

'Me? Why?'

'She doesn't know that many people in Rio and I'm sure she'd enjoy your company a lot more than mine. I'm terribly busy and won't have time to take her around anyway.'

Chantal had no idea what she was getting herself into, but she couldn't very well refuse. 'All right. This is Nelida you're talking about?'

Nelida at twenty-three was his younger sister, single and a schoolteacher in Bahia.

'Yes. And you'll do me a great favour. She'll want to go shopping for Christmas presents and clothes and that sort of thing. A little help would not be amiss. Would you mind?'

'No, of course not. I still have shopping to do myself.'

'Thank you.' He smiled so charmingly that she was beginning to wonder if she had just committed herself to some ordeal she didn't as yet comprehend. Maybe his sister was a pain in the neck, a spoiled brat, an impossible person. She sighed inwardly. There wasn't much she could do about it now.

'When is she coming?'

'She'll be here this afternoon. Would you like to have dinner with us?'

'Can't you handle your sister on your own?'

He grinned. 'I'll need all the help I can get.'

'Mr Hot Shot General Manager doesn't know how to deal with his little sister,' she mocked. 'I guess I'd better come to the rescue.'

He put his hand on his heart. 'You'll have my gratitude forever.' His laughing eyes held hers and again she felt that disturbing stir in her blood and her face went warm under his regard.

I'm falling in love with him, she thought, and the idea

nearly made her panic. She picked up her glass of pineapple juice and took a careful sip, avoiding Enrico's eyes.

I must be out of my mind, she thought. I can't let this happen. I don't want to be in love with anybody. I've had enough of men and their games for a while.

'What's the matter?' he asked softly.

She swallowed. 'Nothing, nothing.' She put down the glass and forced a smile.

He reached across the table and covered her hand with his. 'Your hand is trembling.'

'You're imagining things,' she said lightly, sliding her hand away from under his and trying with all her might to look calm and composed. 'Why would my hand be trembling?'

Nelida had the same dark hair and complexion as her brother, but her eyes were a startling blue—clear and sparkling with some inner joy. Her red mouth, full and generous, smiled at Chantal.

'I'm so glad to meet you,' she said in English, extending her hand. 'I don't get many opportunities to meet Americans these days.'

Chantal smiled back. 'I'm only half, but I hope it will do.'

'Yes, right, of course! Your mother is French. She's lovely. I met her last year when I came to Rio. She was very kind to me.' She sighed, and her smile widened. 'I'm so excited! I'm sure you can tell—I must sound like a five-year old, but I just love coming here for the holidays. This is such a beautiful place. You should see my room! And I love going shopping here. You like shopping?'

'Let's go inside,' Enrico broke in, ushering the two of them ahead of him through the restaurant doors. Grill Boa Vista was one of the Palácio's several restaurants and the Maitre d' was all chic formality, taking no chances with the GM and his guests. They had the very best table with a panoramic evening view of the hills and the city. Drink orders were taken immediately.

Nelida was taking it in with barely contained excitement. She wore a simple white dress, gold earrings and a gold chain necklace. Her hair curled down to her shoulders and she looked beautiful and very young.

'You like to shop?' she asked again. She was a veritable waterfall of enthusiasm, talking in long rambling sentences she had sometimes trouble finishing.

Chantal listened, smiled, nodded, said, yes she'd love to go Christmas shopping with Nelida, and no she had no idea what Nelida should buy for her brother.

Her brother. Chantal glanced over at Enrico, who sat back in his chair, savouring his drink, saying not a word, letting his sister's prattle flow where it might. Good lord, this vivacious, open woman was Enrico's sister? How was such a thing possible? Then she smiled inwardly. Well, she and her own sister formed quite a contrast too.

Enrico's eyes met hers. There was a dark gleam of laughter in his eyes, and it was no secret why he was amused. No secret why he had invited her to come along to dinner. Poor Enrico. His sister probably drove him crazy.

Poor Enrico, indeed! she thought. What about me?

'Enrico says I should buy a new dress for the Christmas party. Do you think it's necessary? I mean, the one he bought for me last year is beautiful and it seems sort of silly not to wear it. Do you think people will remember what I had on last year?'

Enrico put his glass down. 'Go buy a new dress, Nelida,' he said patiently. 'Live it up for once. You have to be practical all year—take a break when you're here. Go shopping and enjoy yourself.'

Nelida smiled and spread her hands in a helpless gesture. 'I'm trying to save him money, but what can I do?'

'Go shopping,' Chantal said drily.

'I guess I'll just have to.' Her eyes were laughing as she looked at Enrico. 'And to think that I couldn't stand him when I was younger.'

'Why not?'

'He was so serious all the time. No fun at all. Very, very boring, let me tell you.'

Chantal laughed. Enrico said nothing and simply sat there sipping his drink.

It was a long, leisurely meal of exquisite food, exquisitely presented and served. Nelida talked—about her family in Bahia, about her first-grade students, about the time, four years ago, when Enrico had invited the whole family over to celebrate Christmas in Switzerland.

'I'll never forget it,' she said, sighing with fond remembrance. 'Those mountains! The snow! And the hotel—it was one of those very old ones, like a castle almost, full of antiques and wood-panelling and stained-glass widows. Very regal, you know.'

Enrico said little all evening, asking only a few questions about his mother and grandfather. They were a close family, it was easy to tell, and Enrico, who had made it big and travelled the world, was still very much involved with them.

A man of loyalty. A man who made strong ties. More pieces to the puzzle.

She glanced at him and his eyes caught hers and he smiled. She'd been aware of him watching her and his sister while they were eating and talking. What was he looking for? she wondered. What was he thinking? Again she felt a restless stirring inside her, a slowm warm excitement. I don't want to fall in love with him! she thought. Please don't let me fall in love with him!

'This is the most delicious dessert I've ever had!' Nelida said, spooning away a brandied peach compote.

'Have another one,' Enrico suggested.

'Oh, no, I couldn't! I'm so full, it's disgraceful. I hope I didn't embarrass you by being such a glutton.'

'I'll get over it,' he said blandly.

Nelida gave him a wounded look, but laughter won out. 'You're awful,' she said, and he gave her a wolfish grin in return.

The lift stopped at Nelida's floor first. She hugged Enrico and thanked him profusely, smiled widely at Chantal and wished them both goodnight. Chantal bit her lip and glanced at Enrico, who was studying her face. Then he laughed.

'That, my dear Chantal, was my sister.'

'I knew you had something up your sleeve when you asked me to keep her company. You should have given me some warning.'

'You would have gone running.'

She grinned. 'True.' The lift door stopped. 'It's my floor,' she said. 'We passed yours.'

'So we did.' He followed her out. 'I'm going to escort you properly to your door.'

They walked down the silent, carpeted corridor to her corner suite. She took her key out of her evening bag and he took it from her fingers and opened the door.

'Thank you for a lovely dinner,' she said, 'even though you did have ulterior motives for asking me.'

He smiled crookedly. 'I do apologise for that. And I thank you for coming.' He paused, holding her gaze. 'You were wonderful tonight. Thank you.'

She felt the heat creep into her face at the look in his eyes. He's going to kiss me, she thought, and her heart began to race.

I don't want him to kiss me. I don't want him to.

Yes, you do, you do, you do . . .

He rested his hands lightly on her shoulders and drew her closer. His head bent towards hers and she closed her eyes. His mouth touched hers, brushing across her lips in a soft, sensuous caress. Not a kiss, not really a kiss, she thought wildly, her lips parting in voluntary response.

His hands slipped up into her hair, cradling her head, and his mouth took hers with firm demand, kissing her with dizzying expertise. Through her thin dress she felt the warmth of his body, only inches away. She wanted to lean into him, feel him against her, but didn't move.

He released her, stepping back. She saw his eyes, dark now, and the rise and fall of his chest. She heard his breathing in the silent corridor and the heavy thumping of her own heart.

'Goodnight, Chantal.' His voice was low and quiet. He turned and strode down the corridor, around the corner and out of sight.

She stared after him, then slowly, as if in a daze, she entered the room and closed the door behind her.

She felt suddenly achingly lonely. The suite was too big, too empty, too perfectly beautiful. It blurred before her eyes as hot tears spilled down her cheeks.

Now why am I crying? she asked herself. Why am I crying?

CHAPTER FIVE

IT WAS ridiculous to be so nervous, but she simply couldn't help it. Stomach tight, heartbeat erratic, Chantal sat cross-legged on a towel on the nearly deserted beach. The morning air felt fresh and clean, but held the promise of summer heat. Restlessly, she peered up and down the beach, looking for Enrico. His towel lay in the sand—at least she assumed it was his—and he had probably gone running as he did most mornings.

One kiss. One kiss that had caused an explosion of feelings in her, feelings she wasn't sure what to do with. She had considered not coming to the beach this morning, to avoid him, but it was impossible. She wanted to see him, be near him.

She didn't have long to wait.

She watched him as he came running towards her and her heart leaped in her chest. It was the most exhilarating feeling, yet it frightened her to feel such overwhelming emotion just seeing him.

One kiss. Just one simple kiss had changed everything. It had revealed to her that there was another, more sensuous part to this glacially controlled man with his cold eyes, a sensuous and sensitive part of which she had caught some glimpses, but now had proof. From that one kiss she knew he would be a wonderful lover, passionate, yet tender and considerate.

Oh, God, she thought, what am I thinking of?

'Bom dia,' he greeted her, wiping his damp hair off his face. His chest was heaving with his laboured breathing and he

grinned as he reached for his towel and wiped his face. 'A run like that does make a man feel alive.'

He certainly did look alive. Wearing nothing but a pair of blue shorts, his lean, muscled body radiated vitality and energy. He settled down on the towel and leaned his forearms on his knees. 'I'll be ready for a swim in a few minutes. Have you been here long?'

'No, just a few minutes.'

They watched the skinny old man doing his exercises. Like the two of them, he was on the beach every morning.

'He must be in his seventies,' Chantal said, trying to find something to neutralise the tension she felt. 'My grandfather is eighty and still plays tennis. Old isn't what it used to be.'

They talked about Enrico's grandfather, about the Christmas party being planned, about Nelida.

Outwardly everything was as it was every morning, but something had changed. There was a new awareness between them. They had entered a new stage in their relationship—a careful reaching out that was frightening and exciting at the same time. She wasn't sure if she was ready for this.

The current between them ran so strong, she felt dizzy with it. There was the absolute conviction that he wanted to kiss her again, that soon she would be in his arms again. It was sweet torture to see him so nearly naked, to know she wanted to touch him. It was the most awkward feeling to pretend everything was as it had been before, to hide her feelings. There was a trembling urgency hidden by casual words, smiles and glances. She found it hard to meet his eyes.

He seemed calm and relaxed, sitting next to her, yet she sensed in him the same feelings, the same restraint of emotion; she could read it in his smiles and in the silvery depths of his eyes. He did not touch her or say anything that referred to the night before, but the knowledge and awareness hovered between them almost tangibly.

They went swimming and the cold water was a relief, cooling her senses and calming her nerves. He moved out behind the breakers with strong strokes and she followed him at a slower pace. She floated on her back, staring up at the delicate blue of the morning sky, wondering what to do.

Nothing. Just let it happen.

She sighed, turned over in the water and swam back to shore.

'That felt good,' Enrico said, coming out of the water five minutes later. He rubbed his hair with his towel. 'Meet you for breakfast?'

It was a little easier to face him across a table, both of them fully dressed, yet the feeling of awkwardness remained and she knew he was aware of her self-consciousness.

'I didn't make a mistake last night, did I?' he asked quietly.

She looked up from the croissant she'd been crumbling between her fingers. Meeting his eyes, she slowly shook her head.

'No,' she said, her voice strangely husky. 'It wasn't a mistake.'

Later that morning, Chantal was dashing off a series of Christmas carols on the piano, feeling light and happy, and waiting for Nicole to join her. She had promised her niece a singing session at the piano to teach her some songs and Nicole had been ecstatic.

She was bubbling with enthusiasm when she came dancing into the bar on the hand of one of the hotel hostesses. Wearing a frilly white sun dress sprinkled with yellow daisies, her dark curls tied back with a long yellow ribbon, her face bright with anticipation, she looked like every mother's dream daughter.

Chantal moved over on the beach to make room and Nicole jumped up next to her with an expectant smile. Chantal kissed her on the cheek. 'I'm glad you're here to sing with me. What shall we sing first? A French song, an English one or a Portuguese one?'

'A French one.'

'OK, and then an English one. Has your *maman* taught you any English Christmas carols?'

Dark curls bounced left to right. *'Non.'*

'OK, I'll teach you one.'

They played and sang. Nicole's voice was clear and confident, if not too tune-steady, but there was no self-consciousness, no shyness. She sat ramrod-straight on the narrow bench, her little legs dangling, her mouth wide open, letting it all hang out. It was a joy to watch.

I want one like her, came the unbidden thought.

'So *this* is what you're doing!' Nelida's laugh was low and amused. 'That horrible man!'

Chantal looked at her, startled. She hadn't heard her coming. 'Hi, Nelida. And what *are* you talking about?'

'Enrico! I asked him if he knew where I could find you, because you weren't in your room. I went to his office and that snotty secretary wouldn't even let me in. Looked me up and down as if I'd crawled from under a rock. She's got this little Christmas tree on her desk, did you see it? Metallic pink with tiny satin bows, really gauche. Anyway, she did check with him when I told her who I was and then she let me go in.' Nelida stopped and laughed. 'I don't know what I was going to say.'

'Something about this horrible man, Enrico.'

'Oh, yes! I asked him if he knew where you were and he said to try the bar. 'The *bar*?' I asked, and he said, 'yes, the bar, that's where she hangs out when she doesn't know what to do with herself. She spends hours there every morning.' Nelida laughed. 'I had the strangest ideas of you . . .' She waved her hand. 'Never mind. Play, play. I want to hear some more.'

They sang, all three of them, in English and Portugeuse and French. They were having a wonderful time. Suddenly, out of nowhere, a deep baritone joined them, and all three of them stopped singing as if on command.

Enrico, grinning, made a nonchalant gesture. 'Sorry if I spoiled the concert.'

'Everybody is always creeping up on me in this place,' Chantal complained.

'Nobody is creeping—you're just too busy to notice anything but that piano when you're playing. So, why don't we sing some more?'

'Not you,' said Nelida. 'You can't sing.'

'What do you mean, I can't sing?'

'You can't hold a note; you never could.'

He looked outraged. 'Do I deserve this? My own little sister, insulting me?'

'I'm not insulting you. I'm just telling the painful truth. Get lost, big brother.'

'Anybody who wants to sing is welcome to sing,' said Chantal. 'Be nice to your brother, Nelida. He's the only one you've got.'

'Wise words from a wise woman.' He grinned smugly. 'Let's sing Jingle Bells.'

Jingle Bells for the fourth time. Chantal groaned inwardly as her fingers hit the keys. They sang, not too harmoniously, but with great enthusiasm. It was an amazing scene to Chantal, sitting here at the piano singing Jingle Bells with Enrico Chamberlain, the same man who had greeted her less than two months ago with his cold smile and wintry eyes.

'And now I'm taking you all to lunch,' he announced when

the song was finished. 'Unless you have other plans.'

'Me too!' Nicole demanded.

'Of course, you too,' he assured her. 'If it's all right with your aunt and mother.'

'Dominique is meeting us in the lobby at one-thirty to pick her up,' Chantal said. 'We have plenty of time.'

It was a lively and enjoyable meal, and Chantal was keenly aware that his attention was centred on her. He was sitting next to her, saying something to her quietly now and then.

'There's a surprise in your room,' he told her as they were sipping their *cafezinho*.

'A surprise?'

He grinned. 'A package.'

'From whom?'

'From me.' His eyes sparked with humour.

'Oh.' She didn't know what to say. She smiled. 'Thank you.'

'You're welcome.'

'I wouldn't trust him if I were you,' Nelida said, having stopped talking long enough to overhear their exchange. 'He's up to something.'

'You're not kind,' Enrico said reprovingly.

She smiled sweetly. 'I'm your sister. I know you.'

Nicole demanded another dish of ice-cream, which she was refused. She pouted for a moment, but was distracted by the promise of looking at the Christmas tree in the hotel lobby.

'Is this the biggest tree in the world?' she wanted to know when they stood looking at it. She craned her neck and gazed at the huge, glittering tree.

'Probably,' Enrico said.

'Is that a real angel on the top?'

'It's a pretend angel.'

'Oh, it's pretty. I like . . .' The words trailed away, her little legs gave way and she slumped to the cold marble floor.

Chantal's heart leaped into her throat. 'Nicole!' She dropped down on her knees, watching in frozen horror as Nicole's arms and legs twitched uncontrollably and saliva drooled from her mouth.

'Don't touch her!' Enrico gently turned Nicole's face to the side. 'Just leave her.'

'Oh, my God,' whispered Nelida. 'I'll go and get a doctor.' She rushed away before either of them could say anything.

It was the longest minute Chantal had ever endured. After the first few seconds of shock she had known instantly what was wrong. An epileptic fit—at least it had all the signs of one. She had never seen one before, but her father had a couple of patients with epilepsy and she knew the signs.

Nicole's body went limp. She closed her mouth, but her eyes still seemed unfocused.

'*Maman,*' she whimpered. 'I want my mommy.'

'It's all right,' Enrico said quietly, reaching out to her and gently lifting her into his arms. 'She'll be here in a moment.'

As if on cue, Dominique appeared at their sides, her face ashen.

'What's the matter with her? What did you do to her?' There was a note of hysteria in her voice. 'Give her to me!' She reached out and Enrico handed her the child. Dominique glared at him wild-eyed. 'What were you doing with my daughter? Why was she on the floor?'

'She had a fit,' he said calmly.

'You're crazy!' Dominique shouted, all semblance of composure gone. Chantal came to her feet, her legs shaking, her heart still beating erratically.

'It's true, Dominique,' she said. 'But she's all right now. Just disorientated.'

Dominique seemed not to have heard. 'Stay away from my child!' she shrieked at Enrico.

Chantal had had enough. Everything had happened in a matter of minutes and they had not attracted any attention, but with Dominique shouting insults at Enrico it wouldn't take long before they drew an audience. She squeezed her sister's shoulder, hard. 'Stop it!' she said with quiet force. 'Calm down! The doctor will be here in a minute.'

Moments later, the hotel doctor, a short, thin Brazilian of Japanese descent, came rushing across the lobby with amazing speed with Nelida in tow.

In a few short sentences, Enrico explained what had happened. 'Let's go somewhere more private,' he suggested and they all followed him into a sitting-room off the lobby.

Dominique was quiet now, but her face was wet with tears. She sat down on a chair after she had laid Nicole down on the blue velvet couch so that the doctor could examine her. Chantal felt sorry for her sister. Nicole meant everything to her and her concern was understandable. Why she had shouted at Enrico as if he were personally responsible was less understandable.

She leaned back in her chair and closed her eyes, listening to the doctor, who was explaining to Dominique that Nicole was all right, but that she needed to go to the hospital for an EEG, a brain-wave test that would show whether Nicole suffered from epilepsy, or if something else was the cause. If it were epilepsy, which he strongly suspected, there was medicine to control the fits.

Maman had been alerted and she came hurrying through the door, her face white and concerned. Once more the story was related.

Enrico met Chantal's eyes. 'Let's go,' he said quietly. 'Your mother will go with Dominique. Come to my office and I'll get us a drink.' He took her hand and drew her out of the chair. His hand was large and warm and he squeezed hers before releasing it.

'I'm not much of a drinker,' she said as he closed his office door behind them. 'It's only two in the afternoon.'

'A glass of cognac will do you good.' He opened a door, revealing a fully stocked bar with a sink and a small refrigerator. He poured them each a glass and she sipped hers slowly. The glow of the spirits spread through her and it did have a calming effect. She sighed. 'This is good.'

'Even at two in the afternoon.'

'This afternoon, anyway.' She met his eyes. 'I'm sorry my sister made such a scene. She was incredibly rude to you.'

'There's no need for you to apologise for your sister, Chantal.'

'She was upset.'

'I know she was upset.' His voice was cool. 'She also doesn't like me very much, which caused that outburst. Let's forget it, all right?'

She surveyed his face for a moment. 'You don't want to tell me what happened between you, is that right?'

He nodded. 'That's right. If you want to know, ask Dominique.'

'I did. She won't tell me.'

He gave a humourless laugh. 'I'm not surprised.'

The mood had soured between them, as it always did when the subject of Dominique entered the discussion. She felt oddly sad. She sipped the cognac in silence, put her glass down on a small table and came to her feet.

'I think I'd better go now. I'm sure you're busy.'

He stood in front of her and smiled crookedly. 'Go up to your suite and find your surprise. Maybe that will cheer you up.'

Surprise. She'd forgotten all about it. She began to smile. 'All right, I'll do that.'

For a moment neither of them moved. Then he leaned his head towards her and touched her mouth to his.

'You'd better go,' he said huskily, and opened the door.

The princess was at her desk. She gave Chantal a waspish look, which Chantal ignored as she crossed the outer office.

Back in her room, she found, on the coffee-table, a small brown paper bag. No fancy box with ribbons—just a brown paper bag. Chantal smiled as she reached for it. It was heavy. She opened it and looked inside. A can. A can of something. She reached in and took it out and stared at it for several seconds. It was a can of Libby's pureed pumpkin and the label had a picture of a pumpkin pie on the front and the recipe on the back. Every year at this time she bought identical cans in the supermarket at Perrydale to make pumpkin pie.

Where had Enrico found this can? Here, in Rio de Janeiro?'

There was a small note attached to the top of the can and she unfolded it and read it.

> *You said you missed having your own kitchen so you could make pumpkin pie. Well, here's the pumpkin and you may use my kitchen at your convenience. The only condition is that you share the pie with me and Nelida. E.*

She smiled at the can like a fool. It would be the best pumpkin pie she would ever make.

Nelida looked wonderful, and she knew it. Her eyes danced with delight as she examined herself in the long mirror. The flirty little dress of black silk chiffon was an ingenious blend of chic and naughty. The strapless fitted top joined a short, layered skirt that swirled sensuously around her upper legs as she moved.

'I love it,' she whispered. 'It's gorgeous!'

Chantal nodded. 'I think so, too.'

'You think I should buy it?'

'Of course you should buy it.'

Nelida searched for the tag. 'How much is it?'

'Don't even look. Just buy it.'

Nelida found the tag and moaned. 'I can't do that. It's awful. It's decadent. I can't spend that kind of money on a dress.'

'You don't have to. You have a rich brother who's doing it for you.'

Nelida sighed. 'Doesn't it bother you, ever, to spend so much money just on clothes?' The question wasn't meant to be as tactless as it sounded and Chantal, taking no offence, laughed.

'I had a lot of practice.'

Nelida stared at herself in the mirror, her eyes wistful; then a smile broke through. 'All right, I'll get it!'

'Good for you. It's the right dress for you, the best we've seen all afternoon.' It fitted her open, artless personality perfectly, the black silk giving it just enough elegance to balance the playfulness of the design.

They spent the rest of the hot afternoon buying shoes to match and some Christmas presents for friends and family. To rest their tired legs they sat down on the shaded terrace of an outdoor café and celebrated the successful afternoon with a *cafezinho* and sweet coconut cakes.

'Sometimes I feel bad about accepting all this from Enrico, you know,' Nelida said, staring across the street shimmering in the summer heat. 'But he wants so very much to give it.'

'Then it shouldn't make you feel bad accepting it.'

Nelida looked at Chantal. 'But he's always giving, giving.' She hesitated. 'He bought a house for my mother, put my sister and me through school. Gave us that trip to Switzerland. He's asked me to come to Rio for the holidays twice now, buys me all these clothes and jewellery.' She fell silent and stared in her cup.

'Why does that make you feel bad?'

Nelida bit her lip and tears welled in her eyes. 'I have nothing to give him back. Don't you see? I have nothing to give him back.' She looked away, embarrassed.

'He's not being so generous just to get something back from you, Nelida,' Chantal said quietly. 'Except maybe to know that he makes you happy by doing it. Maybe he doesn't just give for you; maybe he gives for himself.'

'For himself?'

People were generous for a reason. There was always a reason or a payoff, some way or another. Her mother and grandparents were great givers. Her mother had tried to assuage her guilt for leaving; her grandparents were generous to assure themselves of her love and loyalty to her French family, although they would never, ever admit to attempting to buy her love. They might not even be aware of doing it in any conscious way. She didn't know what Enrico's reason was, but there was one.

'Maybe he does it because it makes him feel good.'

There was a silence as Nelida thoughtfully picked at the cake crumbs on her plate.

'I think Enrico is trying to make it all up to us,' she said after a while.

'Make up what?'

'For what my father did to us. Leaving us with nothing but debts. For what our American grandparents did to us, which was pretend we didn't exist. We weren't good enough for them, you see.' She looked up, her blue gaze searching Chantal's face. 'Do you know about that?'

'Enrico told me a little, just the facts, I think.'

'I wondered if he had. He doesn't talk much, but you're so easy to talk to.' She smiled apologetically. 'I know I talk too much. Do I bore you?'

Chantal smiled. 'I like listening.'

'Why don't you tell me about yourself? I'd like to know. Tell me about when you were little, about your mother and father.'

Nelida seemed truly interested and she listened to Chantal, asking questions, her face intent.

'Do you think you'll stay here in Brazil now?' she asked.

'I don't know,' Chantal said truthfully. 'I may go to France. My grandfather wants me to come, but I haven't decided yet. I'm going to take it easy for a while first.'

'What about your sister?'

'Dominique? She seems to like it here. She does spend a lot of time in France as well, with my grandparents.'

Nelida nodded thoughtfully. 'I hope her little girl is all right.'

'Nicole is fine.' The last couple of days had been rife with worry and tension. Dominique had been in a terrible state, *Maman* was upset, Chantal had worried. Only Nicole had been oblivious, being her happy, cheerful self. The tests had confirmed the earlier diagnosis, but the doctors and specialists had been very reassuring. 'With the medicine they gave her she should be perfectly all right. Epilepsy isn't the terrible thing people used to think it was, you know. She'll be able to lead a normal life.'

Nelida sighed. 'I hope so. She's such a sweet little girl.'

'Yes, she is.' Chantal thought of the terrifying scene in the hotel lobby, of Dominique shouting at Enrico. When the time was right, she would have to talk to Dominique about that. She had been distraught, but that had not been the only reason for her outburst.

It was time to find out what it was that bothered Dominique, and why she hated Enrico.

*   *   *

The party was an annual affair given by Uncle Matteus a few days before Christmas and the guests were friends and business associates. One of the Palácio's large ball-rooms was reserved for the festivities, opulently decorated with silver and crystal ornaments and enormous white flickering candles. Christmas music played discreetly in the background.

The guests themselves were impressive in their array of showy finery, a veritable parade of designer gowns and suits. All colours—raspberry, champagne, fuchsia, cobalt blue, virgin white and basic black; all fabrics—satin, gauze, silk, taffeta and velvet; all lengths—long, mini, and knee. Jewels sparkled and glittered in the candlelight.

'I *love* this!' Nelida whispered to Chantal. *'It's like a movie!'*

Maman floated towards them in a passionate dress of red silk, both hands reached out in greeting, and smiling.

'I'm glad you two are here. You both look lovely.'

'Thank you,' Nelida said, eyes shining. 'Chantal helped me choose it.'

'It's perfect, dear.' Her eyes settled on Chantal, sweeping over the long, slender dress of rich emerald green satin and lace. 'I was hoping you'd wear the green. It really does suit you.'

The lean-cut dress hugged the waist and hips, flaring out below the knee. It had a strapless top with a scalloped and gathered bodice and it fitted her to perfection. She looked glamorous and elegant and not the least bit modest.

Chantal gave her mother a teasing smile. 'I knew you'd like it, *Maman*.'

'I just like you to make the most of yourself, *chérie*. And now you two come with me and I'll introduce you to a few people. And do mingle. There are many people here you'll find interesting.'

Nelida had a wonderful time and soon found herself

entranced by a brawny blond anthropologist who captivated her with the story of his adventures with the Indians in the Amazon interior.

The olive baron Chantal had met at the cocktail party on the day of her arrival attached himself to her, trying to charm her with his wit and knowledge of olives. He was in his late thirties, already greying and quite handsome, but utterly boring. He wondered why Chantal had not accepted any of his invitations. She had been busy, she explained, and very tired, and she usually was in bed by nine, which was the hour civilised Brazilians ate their dinners.

'You go to bed at nine?' he asked incredulously.

She smiled. 'Yes.' It was a lie, but an innocent one, she decided. She was not interested in Jorge and his olives. He seemed to have a hard time grasping that fact, because his persistence over the past weeks had been phenomenal. Listening to him talk, Chantal gleaned the knowledge that Jorge was a very self-absorbed man. He loved himself. He loved his olives. And that was about it.

Gathering all her grace and charm, she excused herself and went in search of Dominique whom she hadn't yet seen. She found her sister at the far end of the ballroom, deep in conversation with a handsome dark man. They were speaking French.

Dominique wore a daring mini of metallic blue, showing off an enviable length of well shaped leg. There was a dusting of glitter in her shiny blonde hair and she looked as if she had walked off the pages of *Vogue*.

'Chantal! Meet Bernard. Bernard Aumont. Bernard, meet my sister, Chantal.'

He smiled a dazzling smile and reached for her hand. *'Enchanté.'* His lips brushed her hand. He was elegant, suave and brimming with Latin charm. Apparently he held some position at the French Embassy, but it wasn't quite clear what.

They exchanged a few pleasantries, after which Bernard offered to get them another drink. Waiters were circulating with trays of glasses of champagne, but neither of them wanted that.

'What do you think of him?' Dominique asked after Bernard disappeared in the direction of the bar.

'Hard to tell after five minutes of polite conversation what's under all that spit and polish. Do you like him?'

'We went out to dinner last night. He's charming and interesting and very available.'

'Is he kind, trustworthy and single?'

Dominique groaned. 'You are such a bore, Chantal. I'm not thinking of marrying the man, for heaven's sake. I've done that routine once and that's enough.'

'Then what *are* you thinking of?'

'Having a good time, what else?'

A good time. Was that all Dominique expected out of life? It was a depressing thought and she was glad when Bernard appeared with their drinks, and two other Charming and Available Young Men in tow.

After fifteen minutes of listening, smiling and sipping her wine, Chantal made her excuses and escaped. She let her gaze travel through the glamorous crowd, looking for Enrico, and finally found him near the buffet table talking to a tall redhead in a ridiculous black and white polka-dot bubble dress. She was looking up at him with wide, adoring eyes and as Chantal came nearer, she heard the affected, girlish laughter.

Enrico's face was a polite mask of utter boredom, to which the redhead seemed oblivious, but his expression cleared when he noticed Chantal. He put his hand lightly on her shoulder. 'Chantal, let me introduce you.'

The redhead was Anita something-or-other, not more than

eighteen or nineteen, and her parents owned a string of posh nightclubs where the rich and famous mingled.

With the subtle skill of long practice, Enrico drew more guests into the small circle, then took Chantal's hand and discreetly withdrew, leaving the bubble dress to the mercies of a bald but bearded politician and his plump wife in pink spangles.

'You want something to eat?' he asked.

She eyed the glorious display of food on the red-draped tables. 'Who can resist?' Platters of the most artistically arranged delicacies tempted the eye as well as the stomach. Huge flower arrangements decorated the table along with tall candles in silver candelabra. 'The only problem is that I don't know what to choose.'

'Try it all.'

'You've got to be kidding! I'll be here till tomorrow noon.' A white-suited waiter handed each of them a large white china plate and they worked their way down the buffet table, loading their plates. After some looking they found a small table for two. A waiter materialised out of nowhere to take their orders for wine.

'I didn't realise how hungry I was,' Chantal said as she began to eat. 'I haven't had anything since lunch and that was almost eight hours ago.'

He watched her with a crooked smile. 'I like to see a woman actually eat. There's nothing more boring than to sit across from a female who eats two lettuce leaves and a carrot because she's on a diet.'

'I'll try and remember that next time I go on a lettuce and carrot binge.'

He looked pained and she laughed. 'You didn't honestly think that I can stow away a plate of food like this with impunity? Sooner or later I have to pay for my sins, just like everybody else.' Not that she had had a lot of problem lately, with her weight way down, but pretty soon she had better start watching it, especially with all the wonderful food that tempted her constantly.

She took a bite of something rich and creamy with crab meat in it. Here we go, she thought, let's enjoy this.

'Talk about sins,' he said, 'when are you going to bake this pumpkin pie?'

After she had found the can in her room she had called him in his office to thank him. 'Nobody ever gave me a can of pumpkin for a present before,' she had said, wondering if his secretary was listening in and wondering what sort of kinky thing they were gong to do with the pumpkin. 'Thank you.'

'You're welcome. Needless to say it was a very selfish gift. I realised it had been years since I'd had pumpkin pie and the memory caused a serious craving.'

'Well, I'll see if I can satisfy that craving. Where did you find it, anyway?'

'Oh, I have my sources.'

'I'll bet. What kind of sources?'

He laughed. 'American friends. They know where to get these things.'

'Very nice of them to help you out. It's also very nice of you to offer your kitchen, but I could use the kitchen in my sister's apartment, if you'd rather. I hadn't even thought of that.'

'No. I insist you use mine.'

She smiled into the phone. 'I'm a very messy worker. Your kitchen may never be the same again.'

'I'll take the risk.'

She wiped her mouth with her napkin and looked across the table at Enrico. 'What's a good time for you?'

'How about six in the evening tomorrow? I'll help you and afterwards we can to to La Sireuse for seafood.'

'It's a deal. I love seafood.'

She looked down on her plate and selected a stuffed mushroom. 'Food for the gods, this. Where did you find a chef you can cook like this?'

'France, where else?'

'Tell me the Executive Housekeeper is German.'

He smiled. 'Of course, and the *maître d'hôtel* is Italian.'

'Almost perfect.'

'Almost? No better than the Italians.'

She looked at him levelly, trying not to smile. 'The ideal hotel has a Swiss GM, surely you were aware of that? How does it make you feel to be the flaw in the set-up at the Palácio?'

He threw back his head and laughed. It was a warm, genuinely amused laugh and it gave her pleasure to see him give in to his merriment so spontaneously.

'I'm afraid I'm merely a poor fake—trained in Switzerland but not the real thing. Just don't tell anybody.'

She smiled into his laughing face, feeling a delicious warmth stirring inside her, and then, as his eyes held hers, she felt her face blush with betraying colour. She picked up her glass and sipped her wine.

'I've been wondering,' she said casually. 'I can understand how you made it from Harvard to Switzerland, but . . .' She stopped, feeling awkward. How was she going to say this delicately? She had wondered how he had managed to get into Harvard all the way from Brazil with not a penny to his name.

'But what?'

'I don't mean to be indiscreet, but I just wondered how you made it to Harvard.'

The corners of his mouth turned down. 'The right name, the right address, the right help. Not necessarily in that order. And scholarships, of course.' He finished his wine and put down the glass, twisting the stem between his fingers. 'I had the incredible luck of having an American businessman taking an interest in my education. I wasn't making a good adjustment to my Brazilian school and he arranged for me to go to the American School here in Rio, and then helped me apply for Harvard.' His mouth twisted. 'Needless to say, my name was a big plus. The only positive thing my father left me.'

Chantal studied his face. It looked cool and composed. 'Did you ever see your grandparents when you were back in New England?' she asked softly.

'No.' He leaned back in his chair and his eyes were steely. 'When I got my MBA, I received a very formal letter from my grandfather inviting me to appear at his office for a business interview.'

She stared at him in amazement. 'After twenty-odd years, your grandfather sent you a *business letter*?'

'That's right. On the company stationery. Very formal, with not a personal word at all.' He shrugged indifferently. 'Needless to say, I didn't reply.'

'Why did he want an interview with you?'

'The right name, the right university, the right degree,' he said cynically. 'I wouldn't be surprised if he had known all along I was at Harvard and had kept track of my performance. In his eyes I had redeemed myself and I could now be allowed back into the family and make my contribution to the family business.'

'That's contemptible!'

'Right.' He picked up the wine bottle and refilled her glass. 'Let's not spoil this food with talk of my American relatives.'

He was a very proud man, she realised. He had rejected an opportunity to become part of the family company, to have his rightful inheritance restored to him, to share in the family wealth. Lesser men would have decided to let bygones be bygones and jump at the opportunity.

Chantal managed to eat her way through her entire plate of food. It was simply too delicious to leave anything. The wine, too, was the best.

'It's probably Brazilian,' Enrico said.

'It's French, read the label.' She gestured at the bottle.

He shook his head. 'You poor, naïve thing. Brazil has some excellent wine and some of it is exported to France and Italy where it's mixed with local grapes, then bottled under a French or Italian label and exported again.'

Chantal laughed. 'And all the poor suckers of tourists pay high prices for French wine while they could be drinking the local stuff.' She placed her hand over her heart. 'From now on, I'll only drink the real thing—Brazilian wine.'

She had never in her wildest dreams expected to be sitting here with Enrico making small talk in such a relaxed casual way, to feel so at ease with him. Sometimes it amazed her she was talking to him at all. There had been nothing inviting about his cold welcome when she had arrived at the Palácio.

'Would you care for some dessert?' Enrico asked and she shook her head. 'I can't eat another bite, but I'd like some coffee.'

People had spotted Enrico and stopped at their table to chat—businessmen, and elegant women on the hunting trail who gave Chantal cool and suspicious looks.

It didn't take long before Enrico seemed to have had enough.

'Let's get out of here.' He frowned and looked at her. 'Sorry,' he said then, 'I didn't mean to imply you should leave the party. Do you enjoy this sort of thing?'

'Usually, for a couple of hours. After a while it gets too much—too many people, too much noise, too much energy floating around.'

'Is there too much floating around now?'

She smiled. 'Definitely.'

'Would you like to find a quieter spot? How about a walk on the beach?'

She looked down at her long dress and high-heeled shoes. 'I don't think I'm dressed for the beach.'

'We can change. How about if I meet you in twenty minutes by the fountain in the lobby?'

Chantal had not been to the beach at night before, and it was an intriguing sight. Here and there, candles flickered in the sand and food and flowers lay beside the candles.

'They're offerings to Iemanjá, the goddess of the sea,' Enrico explained.

'And who puts them there?'

'Umbanda worshippers. It's a cult thing. We have all kinds of cults here that are mixtures of African religions and Catholicism. The slaves brought their religions and superstitions with them from Africa when they came here to work the sugar plantations, and they never disappeared as they did in the States. There's an incredible amount of folklore in this country—the place is populated with ghosts and gods and witches and weird monsters—if you believe in them, of course.'

'You don't?'

'I grew up in America.'

'Right, and we sacrifice at the altar of money and success.'

He grinned. 'Such a cynical statement.'

'Not cynical. It's the truth, isn't it?'

'I suppose it is.' He stopped and looked out over the dark sea, the waves glowing white as they crested. 'On New Year's Eve there's a special celebration when people come to the beach to give their offerings. It's very dramatic and you shouldn't miss it. We'll go and see it.'

He took her hand and started walking again. His hand felt warm and strong, and her nerves tingled all through her. For a long time, they walked without talking, but it was a comfortable silence. If felt good just to walk here with him in the dark, away from the noise and laughter of the party. The cool sea breeze feathered her face and hair and she smelled the salty tang of the sea air. The sky was very clear and stars glowed in the dark.

When was the last time she had walked on a beach at night? It must have been in Cap d'Antibes, years ago, with a young French jazz musician. What was his name? Guy. Guy Moulin. Remembering made her smile. Her grandparents had not approved. Her mother had not approved. The man was rootless, irresponsible, penniless, they said.

'But he's so much *fun*!' she had wailed. He was always telling jokes and thinking up weird schemes. He was different from any man she had ever known and it had been a marvellous, romantic summer. It had stayed that way. He had never written, as he had promised. Not even a card.

'Of course not,' Dominique had said when she had come to Perrydale for Christmas that year. 'He doesn't know how to write. The man is illiterate.'

With David she had never been to any beach, day or night. He liked city life and city entertainment.

David. It had been six months since she had last seen him and she could think of him now without pain. It had all been a mistake and it was over. She could think of the future now without feeling the misery of lost dreams.

'We'd better get back,' Enrico said, and they turned and began to retrace their steps.

'Do you often go walking on the beach at night?' she asked,

and he smiled.

'Two, three times a week probably. It helps me relax and clear my mind.'

'Like me and the piano.'

'Yes.'

'There's something I'd like to ask you.' She hesitated. Maybe she shouldn't. Maybe it was too personal a question.

'All right.'

'You don't have to answer it.'

'All right,' he said again. 'Shoot.'

'Are you happy?'

'Happy? When? Now?'

'No, in general. Are you happy with your life? Are you a happy person?'

There was a silence and she wondered if she had made a mistake.

'I'm content with my life,' he said then. 'I've done what I wanted to do. I'm doing what I want to do.'

He had not strictly answered the question, telling her whether he was happy, but she had her answer anyway. It wasn't a surprise, of course. Despite his high-powered job and all his success, true happiness had escaped him. She wondered if he was a lonely man.

He stopped walking and stepped in front of her. He looked into her eyes, but it was difficult to see anything in the shadowy night. He lifted his hands up and slowly smoothed her hair. Then he lowered them around her back and held her, saying nothing, just looking at her. Her heart began to beat erratically, knowing she wanted him to kiss her, to feel again that passionate demand of his mouth. She wondered what was going on in his mind, what he was thinking of her as he was holding her.

She closed her eyes as his face came closer. Warmth rushed through her as his mouth covered hers. His kiss was warm and gentle at first, a sensual exploration she didn't resist. Then it grew more intense, with a hunger and passion that sent her reeling. His arms grew tighter around her and she felt the tension in his body as it pressed against hers. Her senses swam, and she responded to his kiss with a yearning she couldn't suppress.

Finally he let go of her mouth, drawing her face against his shoulder and just held her. She could feel the thumping of his heart—or was it her own? It took moments before her heart began to slow its frantic beating and her breathing was half-way normal again. He released her slowly, looking into her eyes again.

'What about you?' he asked. 'Are you happy?'

'I'm working on it. I intend to be.'

'You will be,' he said, and smiled. He took her hand again and they continued their walk.

She was glad he didn't ask her how she was working on it. She wasn't sure how to answer that. It was only recently that she had started to give some serious consideration to her future. Should she go to France? Stay here in Rio? What about her feelings for Enrico? Was it worth staying for and taking the risk of another loss? Another disappointment? There was so little she knew about him, yet her feelings were so strong, they frightened her.

They walked on in silence, their hands locked together, and the sound of rushing water, the eternal rhythmic motion of the waves seemed to envelop them, creating a private place where no other thoughts seemed relevant or necessary. At least not for now, for tonight.

Entering the hotel lobby with its waterfall, crystal chandeliers and enormous glittering Christmas tree was like stepping into another world.

'You want to go back to the party?' Enrico asked.

She laughed, looking down at her jeans and shirt and sandy

feet. 'Like this?'

He grinned. 'No, I suppose not.'

He took her up to her suite. At the door he took her into his arms and kissed her, then released her. He smiled down at her face. She wondered if he was waiting for her to ask him in. She wanted him with her, yet the words didn't come.

'May I come in?' he asked quietly, and again her heart began to pound wildly—with a mingling of fear and excitement. She knew what he was asking. She knew that if she let him in, he would not leave again.

The urgency to touch him was so strong she found herself tense with the effort not to reach out, her hands clenched hard, her muscles taut. She felt a terrible hunger for his touch, a deep yearning to be held and kissed and made love to.

'Yes,' she said softly.

CHAPTER SIX

HE PUT his arm around her shoulders and moved her through the door into the dark room. She felt like an awkward schoolgirl and she reached out to turn on a light, but he captured her hand in mid-air and drew her into his arms. The wild rhythm of her heart seemed to fill the room. His lips caressed her temple, her cheek, her chin with slow sensuous touches. She stood very still, barely breathing now, savouring his touch.

'Play the piano for me,' he whispered in her ear.

'The piano?' She drew back, uncomprehending. It wasn't what she had expected to hear. 'I don't . . .'

'Look to your left.'

She moved her head. There, in the far end of the room, awash in pale moonlight that shimmered through the big arched windows, stood a piano.

'You got me a piano?' she whispered.

'Compliments of the Palácio, for your personal use and my personal enjoyment.' His mouth tilted in a smile. 'I don't want to have to sneak off to the bar in the middle of the morning to listen to you.'

She laughed softly. 'You are full of surprises.'

'You mean this is not what you expected when I asked to come in?'

'No,' she said, trying not to smile. 'I thought you might want to look at my etchings.'

'There are no etchings in this suite.'

'Oh, heck,' she said blandly and he gave a low rumble of a

laugh.

His lips feathered across her mouth. 'Play for me.' His arms dropped away from her and she moved over to the piano. The furniture had been rearranged to accommodate it and she noticed the changes now that her eyes had adjusted to the dark. It wasn't really so dark with the moonlight spilling in through the windows. She sat down on the bench and switched on the light. Her fingers slipped on to the keys and began to move as if of their own volition, playing Debussy's *Clair de Lune*. Enrico stood beside her, watching her, and when she finished she smiled up at him. 'Sounds wonderful.'

'That's what I thought.'

'I meant the piano.'

'I meant your playing.'

'Thank you.'

His laugh was low and amused. 'Where's your music?'

'It's over on the table there.' He handed her the stack of books and sheet music and she searched through them. 'What else would you like me to play? Any particular piece?'

His eyes held hers and a faint smile played around his mouth. 'What about *Liebestraum*, and Beethoven's *Moonlight Sonata*?'

She listened to the silence and watched his face. The most romantic music in the world, and he had asked her to play it for him.

'If you want me to.'

'I want you to.' He lowered his face and touched his mouth to hers. 'Please.'

He straightened away from her and settled himself comfortably in one of the deep, upholstered chairs, stretched out his legs and closed his eyes.

'If you fall asleep, I'll never forgive you,' she said with a laugh.

'Not to worry.'

She played for almost an hour, playing several of Chopin's romantic pieces as well. Enrico said not a word, just quietly sat in his chair, listening with his eyes closed. The room was filled with sound and emotion and she felt herself slip away into that special world where nothing else seemed to touch her; where there were just the two of them in the shadowed room, captured in the magic spell of the music.

She finished with the first movement of the *Moonlight Sonata*, sitting quietly for a moment, before slowly getting to her feet and moving to the window. The moon was almost full, silvering the ocean with its light. She heard him get up and then he was next to her, very close, but not touching.

'Thank you,' he said softly. 'That was wonderful. I could listen to you all night.'

She smiled at him. 'Thank you for the piano.'

He took her hand and lifted it to his lips, kissing each finger with a soft, tender touch. It was, somehow, oddly erotic and she felt her body leap into life.

'Magic fingers,' he said, entwining his fingers with hers.

They stood in silence, looking out over the shadowy hills and the glittering lights of the city hugging the bottom of the slopes. The sound of music still seemed to linger in the room.

'It's such a beautiful city,' she said at last, her voice low and quiet.

'Yes. *A cidade maravilhosa*, as they say.' He turned and slowly drew her into his arms. His mouth found hers and he kissed her again with that heady mixture of passion and tenderness, his arms curving her body against his own.

'I want to make love to you,' he whispered.

'I know.' His words, his closeness made her tremble.

'You're nervous,' he said gently.

'It shows?'

With one finger he traced the outline of her mouth. 'Yes.'

'Maybe I should have a drink.'

'Maybe I should leave.'

She gave a half-smile. 'Don't confuse me. I didn't expect you to be one of those sensitive guys.'

'I just asked you to play me Liszt's *Liebestraum.*'

'Well, yes, that's right.'

'I have a rule.' He trailed his fingers through her hair. 'I don't make love to women who don't want to.'

'I didn't say I don't want to. Not many ever say no, I expect.'

He gave a crooked smile. 'I haven't made love to many women.'

She laughed softly. 'That's not a very macho statement, you knw. Are you sure you're half Brazilian?'

'Quite. But when I do anything, I do it right, or at least I try. When I'm involved, I'm involved. I don't go for fast flings and one-night stands, so you'd better be prepared.'

Nothing half-way with him. She should have known. He had the reputation of being hard to get; there were no stories doing the rounds about his romantic escapades.

'What exactly should I be prepared for?' she asked.

'To take this relationship seriously. To take my feelings for you seriously.'

And what are your feelings for me? she wanted to ask, but she didn't voice the words. It wouldn't be fair to put him on the spot. She wanted to hear it from him when he was ready to tell her, without her prompting. She wasn't ready herself to vocalise her own feelings—they were too tender and new and she wasn't sure how to express them in words . . . not yet, anyway.

'And will you take me and my feelings seriously?'

'Of course.' He cradled her face in his hands and brushed

his lips against hers. 'And you didn't answer my question.'

'What question?'

'Do you want me to leave?'

She met his eyes, feeling a rush of warmth. 'No.'

'You're not nervous any more?'

She shook her head. 'No.'

'Were you worried about my intentions?' He released her face and curved his arms around her back.

'I was worried about the wisdom of the whole situation, of giving in to my own feelings. It's not all that . . . easy for me.'

He held her tightly. 'Will you trust me?"

'Yes,' she whispered. And she felt she could; she felt safe with him, which seemed like a strange revelation.

His mouth nuzzled her neck. 'And now,' he said quietly, 'there is another, more practical consideration. Would you like me to take care of it?'

She gave a soft, surprised laugh. 'You were already planning this night's diversion?'

He held her away from him a little so that he could see her face. 'It doesn't pay to be stupid, Chantal.' He gently touched her cheek with his hand. 'I'm a responsible person, and the idea of making love to you isn't something that just popped into my head when I brought you home tonight.'

'Thank you.' It was all she could say, all that was necessary. His eyes held hers and she felt warm under the intense regard. Both his hands reached up to touch her hair, stroking it slowly.

'I want to make love to you very much,' he said quietly. 'I've wanted to for a long time.'

'Yes.' Her voice was unsteady.

There was tenderness in his eyes. He moved his hands down her back again and he stood there, not moving, just holding her in a gentle embrace, his light eyes turning dark as he gazed into her face.

'You're so beautiful,' he said huskily. 'Such lovely green eyes, such a warm, tender mouth. Kiss me, Chantal.'

His words trembled through her, stirring her blood. Slowly she lifted her arms to hold him, reaching up to touch his mouth. He made a soft sound in his throat, and his arms crushed her closer to him. His mouth took over, hungry and impatient, and fire raced through her. Her heart pounded with wild, laboured beats and she felt giddy with a glorious, sweet excitement. She could feel the tension in his body, the heat of his skin.

He released her suddenly, taking an unsteady step back. His chest was heaving and his eyes were dark and unfocused. He raked his hands through his hair in an oddly uncertain gesture. 'My God,' he muttered, his voice shaken. 'We'd better take this a little slower.'

I don't want to, she said silently. Her tongue refused to move.

He took her hand. 'Come on.' He led her into the bedroom, closing the double doors behind them. The curtains had been drawn, the bed covers turned back. A small lamp had been switched on low and a pink rose lay on her pillow. This was the way she found her room every night.

He undressed her slowly, touching and kissing her softly all over, warm, moist kisses that made her blood sing. His fingers feathered along her skin, sending exquisite sensations quivering through her.

'You're so beautiful,' he said again, darkened eyes sliding over her as she stood naked before him in the muted light. He cupped one breast in his hand and closed his warm mouth over the nipple. A soft moan escaped from her throat and her knees grew weak. She leaned into him, trembling, aching.

'Enrico . . .' She laughed breathlessly. 'I can't just stand here like this with you doing that.'

He laid her down on the bed and quickly worked himself out of his clothes. She had seen most of him at the beach, but now there were no more mysteries left. She swallowed as she watched his brown torso, longing to touch him and hold him against her. She closed her eyes, and then he was beside her on the bed, his hand stroking her belly. She moved on to her side, closer to him, and pressed her mouth against the springy hair on his chest—a solid wall of strength. She wrapped one arm around him, stroking the muscled contours of his back.

They touched and kissed each other, tongues tangling in a primitive dance of desire. She revelled in the taste and scent of him, her senses clamouring. He made her body quiver. He made her sigh and smile and moan with helpless rapture.

'This feels so good,' she murmured. 'So good, so good . . .' she sighed, finding no other words.

'Look at me,' he whispered and she opened her eyes, focusing on his face in the faint rosy glow of the bedside lamp. She had never seen his face like this, the deep, hungry yearning in his eyes. All the hard, angular lines were gone. He touched a finger gently to her lips.

'I want you,' he said huskily. 'I need you.'

'Need me?' The words confused her. He always seemed so self-sufficient, as if he needed no one.

'I need you in my life. I need to be with you and hear your music. You touch my soul with your music, you know that, don't you? When I'm with you, I feel like a different man.' He lowered his head, resting his face against her breast. 'Tell me you want me, tell me you need me too.' His voice was husky with longing.

She laid her hands on the back of his head, burrowing her fingers in the thickness of his hair. 'I need you,' she said softly, holding his head against her breast. 'I want you.' She needed him to be her friend and lover, to be there for her always. She wanted his love and his loving.

He gave a soft groan as he shifted his body, pressing the whole hard length of him against her. She stirred, restless with desire, her body feverish, throbbing.

'Chantal . . .' His body trembled with a driving need. She clung to him and his body melded with hers and all was lost in the wild turbulence of loving until the tension crested like the waves, breaking into shuddering release.

Her body stilled beneath his and he slumped against her. 'Oh, God,' he muttered raggedly. 'I didn't know I could feel this way.'

He took his weight away from her and she nestled her face in the warm hollow between his neck and shoulder, giving a little shiver of delight. 'You made me feel so good,' she whispered, and he laughed softly, his hand languorously stroking her hip and thigh.

'No regrets?'

She lifted her face and smiled into his eyes. 'Oh, Enrico, how can you even ask?'

The next day, Chantal had lunch with Dominique in a small restaurant located in an old colonial house furnished with antiques and exuding the atmosphere of times gone by. Chantal hadn't seen much of her sister since the frightening scene with little Nicole in the hotel lobby, but it seemed that she had pulled herself together and had accepted the inevitable.

Today she was going to ask Dominique about her outburst at Enrico, and what it was that had happened between them to make her so full of hate. It was time to know, yet she didn't relish the discussion. Maybe she had better wait until after they had eaten so at least the meal wouldn't be ruined. There was no doubt in her mind that it wasn't going to be pleasant.

'This is a great place,' Chantal said, glancing around and examining the old prints and oils on the walls.

'Yes.' Dominique studied her face. 'You look marvellous,' she said, 'better than ever in the last couple of months.'

Chantal smiled. 'Thank you. I feel pretty good.' It was an understatement of mammoth proportions. She felt happier than she had ever felt in her life. Last night's love and joy glowed inside her like a slow, warm fire. All morning she had felt almost delirious with happiness.

She and Enrico had not gone swimming that morning but stayed in bed. He had awakened her at six with soft kisses and caresses and they had made love again—a slow, languorous loving that had been so different from the time before, yet with a satisfaction all its own.

They had called room service for a champagne breakfast. Pears poached in port wine, a crab meat and cheese omelette, fresh, hot croissants, mango preserves and *café au lait*. The feast was served on a rolling table set with white Irish linen and Limoges china, and decorated with a single yellow rose. A silver bucket of ice had held a bottle of Brazil's finest champagne.

She had been ravenous and it had been the best breakfast she had ever had, the champagne suiting her joyful mood perfectly. Crab seemed a strange choice for breakfast, but then the English ate kippers, she reminded herself, and in the Far East people ate noodles and pork in the morning. An open mind could lead to great new discoveries.

With an effort she pushed away thoughts of her breakfast with Enrico. She glanced at Dominique. 'I was pretty run down when I arrived here. I didn't know how much I needed a rest.'

Dominique took a sip of her wine. 'You sure looked as if you did.'

Over a plate of *moqueca de peixe*, a delicious Brazilian fish dish, they talked about Nicole, about Christmas, and about Bernard Aumont. Dominique's light-hearted talk of him did not deceive Chantal. Dominique was in love. She was also terrified. Which wasn't such a surprise. A failed marriage didn't do anybody's ego any good.

They had some delicious pastries for dessert along with their coffee and Chantal knew that in a few minutes she would have to ask Dominique to tell her story. She wished she didn't have to do it, but she simply had to know.

Dominique sighed and leaned back in her chair. 'That was good. I shouldn't have had it, but I'll skip dinner tonight. Oh, by the way, I've wanted to ask you, did you ever get any more telexes from that 'M' in Minneapolis?'

For a moment, the old apprehension was back. Chantal shook her head. 'No. I kept worrying about it, and then I forgot.'

'Strange, wasn't it?' Dominique frowned, then shrugged lightly. 'Anyway, I'm glad. Probably just some nut.'

'I guess so.' She wished Dominique hadn't mentioned it. It had been weeks since the telexes had come, but it still made her uncomfortable thinking about them. She forced the issue from her mind.

She pushed her plate away and looked at her sister. 'Dominique, there's something I want to talk to you about.'

Dominique carefully wiped her mouth with her napkin. 'What about?'

'Enrico.'

Dominique's face froze.

Chantal sighed. 'Listen, I know you were terrified when you saw Nicole on the floor in the lobby that day, but you owe Enrico an apology.

'I don't owe him anything!'

'Dominique! You practically *accused* him of hurting Nicole! You were *blaming* him for what happened! Why did you react so strangely? What is it that sets you off?'

'I just can't stand the man.'

It seemed to Chantal, at this very moment, almost an impossibility that anybody could dislike Enrico. The man she now knew, the man she had spent the night with, was the best she had ever known. Yet she remembered her own feelings of dislike, not so very long ago. It was very true indeed that Dominique could not stand Enrico. And that was actually putting it mildly.

She looked at her sister. 'That's an understatement. But even so, that's no reason to say the things you did. He's been wonderful with Nicole. He plays with her, he talks with her—he likes her.'

There was a strained silence. Dominique crumbled a piece of cake and stared at her plate. Finally she looked up.

'I know you've been seeing him,' she said tonelessly. 'As a matter of fact, I believe you're madly in love with him.'

'We aren't talking about him and me.'

'Has he told you anything?'

'No, he hasn't. He told me to ask you.'

Dominique grimaced. 'Such a gentleman,' she said sarcastically.

'Dominique!'

Dominique sighed. 'You're not going to give me peace until I tell you, right? Well, since you're seeing him despite my warning, I suppose maybe it would be better if I told you. It wouldn't hurt for you to know what kind of man he is. But not here.'

'You want to go to my place?'

'Fine. Have you anything to drink up there?'

Chantal shrugged. 'A couple of things. Let's go.'

They were silent all the way back to the Palácio. Dominique seemed uncomfortable and Chantal wondered for the umpteenth time what could have happened to make her beautiful, self-confident sister so uneasy. It took a lot to shake her. Everything in her life had always reinforced her ego—money, beauty, adoring men.

In Chantal's sitting-room, Dominique sat down in a chair, crossing her arms in front of her chest as if she were cold.

'It's a long story.' She bit her lip. 'You know I had a difficult pregnancy.'

'Yes.'

'I suppose I shouldn't have got pregnant so soon after Sergio and I were married, but . . . well, it happened. Actually, I think I really wanted to, and Sergio was happy about it, so it didn't matter.'

'Then what was the problem?'

'I wasn't much of a wife while I was pregnant.'

'What do you mean by that?'

Dominique hugged herself harder. 'I was sick all the time. The doctor gave me every possible medicine that was safe to take and nothing helped. I was always vomiting up my food. I didn't want to go anywhere. I couldn't eat anything. I felt weak and miserable.' There was a pause and Dominique stared out of the window. She was struggling with herself. Finally she glanced back at Chantal, her face contorted. 'I didn't feel like making love any more. I couldn't stand the idea. All I wanted to do when I got in bed was sleep and hope I didn't have to get up before morning.'

'And Sergio didn't understand that?'

'For a while. Then he started turning cool towards me. I think he couldn't stand looking at me any more. I looked awful. I didn't bother to do anything with myself—my hair, my face. All I could think of was how I was going to make it through the day without losing every morsel of food I ate. I was worried about the baby.'

Chantal listened. She hadn't realised it had been that bad. For Dominique not to care about her appearance, it had to be very bad. But what any of this had to do with Enrico, she had no idea, yet she said nothing, not wanting to interrupt.

Dominique chewed on her lip. 'Sergio started going out alone. I couldn't blame him. I didn't want to go, and to make him stay home for me didn't seem fair.' She shrugged fatalistically. 'Not that I could have made him do anything he didn't want to do. He always did as he pleased.'

Chantal felt a rush of indignation. 'Was it fair for you to be alone and sick all the time?'

Dominique shrugged and was silent.

'So what happened?'

'He got himself a mistress.'

Chantal stiffened. Blood ran cold through her veins. 'He got a *mistress* while you were pregnant?'

'He told me he had every right. He didn't see any harm in it.'

'How did you find out, or did he tell you himself?'

'A friend of mine told me, and then I confronted him. He didn't even feel guilty. He said there was no reason why he should deny himself and I had no reason to complain, because it kept the pressure off me.' She gave a bitter little laugh.

'I can't believe this! What did you do?'

'I almost went crazy. I hated him.' She closed her eyes. 'Then I tried not to think about it. I hoped maybe everything would turn to normal after the baby was born. I'd feel like a wife again.'

'You were going to accept it?'

'I didn't know what else to do.' Her mouth twisted. 'You may find this hard to believe, but I loved him. I hated him for what he was doing to me, and I still loved him. Don't ask me why. It's perverse, I know. I don't understand it myself.'

Chantal stared at her sister in silence. It was incomprehensible to hear this story from Dominique, who in the past would never put up with any such men. A proud woman who was not used to compromises, who did not take second best, who did not deny herself. Was this what love did? Make you crazy? Lose all sense of proportion? Make you accept the unacceptable?

A thought occurred to her. Maybe she, Chantal, had not loved David enough. His accusation still echoed in her mind. If you truly love me, you would forgive me.

She had not forgiven him his deception, his lies.

And she wasn't sorry, now. Maybe she hadn't loved him enough. She wanted truth and honesty. Nothing else would do.

'So what happened after Nicole was born?'

Dominique gave a humourless laugh. 'He was disappointed she wasn't a boy, to start with, but he did know his biology so he couldn't accuse me of falling down on the job. I tried to make the best of it. Physically I started feeling better right away. I could eat again and I started looking better. I spent all kinds of time and money on myself. Exercised to get my shape back, got new clothes, tried to be happy and cheerful.'

'Did it work?'

'No. He was too involved with his mistress.' Dominique's face was bleak, her voice bitter. 'He didn't want me any more.'

This, in the final analysis, must have been the greatest blow of all. Dominique had no experience in rejection; it was not something she knew how to cope with.

She covered her face with her hands. 'I did everything, everything, and I simply left him cold. Oh, God, Chantal, you don't know what I went through.'

'It must have been terrible.' It sounded hopelessly inadequate, but she couldn't think of anything else to say. She was appalled that she had never known the extent of Dominique's misery. Her pride had kept her silent; she hadn't wanted anybody to know, not even her own sister.

'I wanted him to love me again, but he only looked at me as if he pitied me. He made me feel cheap and dirty and I hated him. I was beginning to doubt myself. I was beginning to think something was wrong with me, that I wasn't attractive any more or desirable or just not . . . worthy of a man's love.' Her voice broke. 'It . . . it was the most awful feeling.' Tears filled her eyes and for a moment she said nothing, swallowing at her tears and seeing things in her mind Chantal could only guess at. She felt compassion rise in a wave of love. More than four years ago and still it made Dominique cry.

Dominique went into the bathroom and blew her nose.

'Damn,' she said, as she came out again. 'I don't know why I do this.' Her mouth trembled. 'I have never told this to anybody.'

'Maybe it was time.'

'Don't bottle it all up and all that.' She plopped herself back down in the chair in a rather inelegant fashion and pulled up her knees. 'Now comes the good part,' she said derisively. 'I really lost it and I did something incredibly stupid. I've often wondered how I could have been so utterly brainless, but you have to take into consideration that I wasn't rational at the time. I was nothing but a bundle of nerves and emotion and negative feelings. I wanted to do something. I wanted to know I was still woman enough to attract a man.'

Chantal closed her eyes and sighed. 'And you went for Enrico.'

'Yes,' she whispered.

'Why Enrico, of all men?'

'I knew him and he was single and handsome and I loved that go-to-hell look of his and he had the reputation of being very hard to get.'

Chantal groaned, but couldn't suppress a smile. Trust her sister to take up an impossible challenge. Tell her she couldn't have something and she went after it with a vengeance. 'You didn't just want to prove yourself, Dominique, you wanted to prove yourself in the most difficult way possible.'

'I didn't think of it that way at the time, but I suppose that's true. Only it didn't work.'

'So what happened?'

Dominique hesitated, her face agonised. 'Chantal, will you promise never to tell this to anyone, not ever?'

'Of course I won't.'

Dominique closed her eyes and sighed. 'Oh, God, this is so humiliating.'

Chantal wasn't sure she wanted to hear any more, yet she sensed that it was necessary for Dominique to get it out of her system, to purge herself of all the bottled-up anger and to come to terms with herself. It was what her father had always said: *Sometimes the best medicine is just to talk and have somebody listen.* All right, she would listen.

Dominique took in a deep, steadying breath. 'I'd tried for a few weeks to attract his attention, but he seemed rather cool and distant. Well, you know how he is. I wondered if I was being too subtle, or if behind that impenetrable demeanour of his he was not as secure as you might expect from a man like him. I came up with all sorts of reasons. I didn't want to accept that maybe he wasn't interested. I couldn't afford to think that.' She swallowed hard. 'Then there was a party at his apartment, and *Maman* and Uncle Matteus and I were invited. Sergio was in Buenos Aires on business.'

Dominique stared out of the window, her face blank. 'I

didn't go home, but stayed on until everyone had left,' she said in a monotone. 'I went to his bedroom.'

'To his *bedroom*?'

'Don't make it harder for me than it already is, please. Yes, his bedroom. I sat down on the bed and waited.'

Chantal could not believe what she was hearing. Her proud, beautiful sister, who had never had any shortage of handsome men vying for her attention, had thrown herself in the most blatant fashion at Enrico. There was a pause, but she said nothing, just waited.

'He seemed surprised when he saw me,' Dominique went on. 'He asked me what I was doing in his bedroom.' She licked dry lips. 'So I told him. I went up to him, put my arms around him and . . . and kissed him.' She swallowed hard. 'He . . . he grabbed my shoulders and pushed me away and made me sit on the bed while he stood in front of me, looking down on me with that face of stone and told me what he thought of me.'

She took a deep shuddering breath. 'Chantal, I have never been so humiliated in my life. I would have gladly died right then and there.'

Chantal could visualise the scene in Enrico's bedroom, see his face, hear the tone of his voice. She had an idea of what he had said. She didn't need to ask.

'Every time I see him,' Dominique continued, 'I think of that night. I can't help it. I can't forget it.'

Rejection and humiliation by two men in a row, and one of them her husband. It had not been an easy time for Dominique. It was not surprising, Chantal thought, that she was so bitter and angry even now.

'I'm sorry,' she said softly. 'I wish you would have told me sooner. Why didn't you ever tell us? Don't you think Dad . . .'

'Oh, Chantal, get real! Can you imagine me telling this sorry tale to *Dad*? That quiet, pious, fuddy-duddy doctor?'

'Yes, I could have imagined that. You have no idea what stories he heard, the things people told him. You might have been surprised at what he would have said.'

Dominique was quiet for a moment, her face oddly wistful. 'You did know him a lot better than I.'

'I lived with him. Of course I knew him better.'

The next morning Chantal and Enrico went swimming as usual and afterwards they sat in the sand for a while, watching the joggers go by. Chantal was preoccupied with the story Dominique had told her the day before and said little. She wasn't sure if she should mention it to Enrico, or just forget it. It wasn't her problem. It had nothing to do with her.

'You're quiet this morning,' he commented.

She took a handful of sand and let it flow out slowly over her leg. 'Dominique told me yesterday.' There was no need to say what it was her sister had told her.

'Let's hope it made her feel better,' he said coolly.

She said nothing and gazed at the glittery sand.

'What are you thinking?'

'I'm just wondering why you couldn't just have sent her away without humiliating her so.'

'Your sister was having a hard time understanding my more subtle signals. She'd been after me for weeks.' His tone was impatient. 'I decided to be blunt and to the point so there would be no more doubt.' He paused fractionally. 'I don't abide women who cheat on their husbands or husbands who cheat on their wives.' His voice was cold and hard.

'Did you have to humiliate her?'

He frowned impatiently. 'She was *asking* for it, for God's sake! She was in my bedroom, uninvited, and made me a proposition she thought I couldn't refuse. Your sister is a spoiled, selfish woman who thinks she can have whatever she wants. Well, she couldn't have me.'

Chantal was trembling with anger. 'She also couldn't have her own husband, the man she was married to legally! *He* found himself a mistress while she was pregnant and sick!' She swallowed. 'You had no right to be cruel to her. No person has the right to be cruel to another human being!'

'I admire your loyalty,' he said coolly.

'You're a bastard,' she whispered fiercely. She leaped to her feet and swept her towel up from the sand, afraid of the terrible anger lodged in her chest. She turned away from him, not wanting to see the cool indifference in his eyes. Not wanting to see him at all.

CHAPTER SEVEN

SHE lurched away, almost losing her balance when he grasped her arms and jerked her back down in the sand next to him.

'Am I?' he asked, his voice tight. His eyes bored into hers and she glared back at him, rigid with resentment. She remembered the time she had come to his office to see if he would help her find a job; she remembered the condescension, the sarcasm.

She yanked herself free from his grasp. 'Yes,' she said through clenched teeth. Yet it was only part of the truth. She knew the other side of him—the warm, loving part of him, and it was difficult to imagine that those two so contradictory character traits belonged to the same man.

'If I am,' he said, 'then it is because I had to be. I learned the hard way that when there are problems it's better to be tough and deal with them. Being nice because you don't want to be tough and deal with them. Being nice because you don't want to muddy the waters usually doesn't get you anywhere.' He searched her face. 'Chantal, I am not where I am because it was given to me on a silver platter. I did not succeed because I was lucky. I am the General Manager of the Palácio because I worked for it. I did it myself, and it was never easy and maybe it didn't make me a very nice person.'

'And you resent people like Dominique and me because we were born into money and didn't have to work for it.'

'I was born into it too,' he said bitterly, 'but in the wrong family.'

'And now you despise everybody with "born" money, don't

120

you? That's why you didn't like me when I first arrived.' She stopped, hearing her own words echoing back to her. It was suddenly so very clear. It amazed her she hadn't thought of that angle before. 'I was just another spoiled little rich bitch, wasn't I? You weren't even prepared to give me the benefit of the doubt! Well, I'm not my sister and not all wealthy families are like yours, Mr Chamberlain!' She leaped to her feet, plodding inelegantly through the soft sand, hoping he wouldn't follow her and see her tears of anger and frustration.

He could be so hard and unfeeling. How could she ever learn to deal with that?

She had breakfast sent up to her room, studied some Portuguese and spent an hour with her tutor in one of the meeting-rooms off the lobby. She went back to her rooms and sat down at the piano. She stared at the keys, remembering the feelings of the night they had spent together, the music and the loving, and she slammed her hands down on the keys, her senses screaming in protest at the awful cacophony.

'Oh, damn you!' she muttered fiercely. She pushed the bench back violently. She couldn't play.

She ordered coffee and watched a horror movie on television. She never watched horror movies, but for some perverse reason, she did now.

The phone rang just as she was ready to go out to lunch with Nelida and her mother. It was her grandmother.

'Just a call to see how you are doing, *chérie*.'

'I'm fine, *Grand-mère*, and you? Is your arm all right?'

Three months ago her grandmother had fallen, not breaking a hip, as she was supposed to at the age of seventy-nine, but an arm.

'It's as good as it ever was.'

'I'm glad.'

They talked for about ten minutes, mostly about Nicole, and

then her grandfather came on the line.

'Have you thought about it?'

'About what?' she asked, feigning ignorance.

'About returning to France!' he roared. 'About going to work for me!'

'What about Uncle Albert? And what do Jean Jacques and Bertrand think of the idea?'

'I didn't ask them!'

'Don't you think you should?'

'No, I don't think I should! As long as I am running the company, they'll damn well think what I tell them to think!'

She bit her lip. 'I see.' This situation promised nothing good. The last thing she wanted was to be the cause of a major family crisis. Knowing her uncle and cousins, she wasn't sure they would receive a half-foreign female relative into the company with open arms. She was certainly part of the family, but entering into the family business was something altogether different.

So far, she hadn't really taken her grandfather seriously, thinking he would change his mind, or he would be talked out of it by his son and grandsons. Now she wasn't so sure.

'*Grand-père*, I don't know that I want to, but I certainly don't want to if it means problems with Uncle Albert and the cousins.'

'There won't be any problems.'

'How do you know that if you haven't talked to them?'

'I know! I'm the boss! I run this outfit! They do what I say!'

She doubted that this really was the case. Her uncle and cousins were no meek lambs by any stretch of the imagination. The idea that they were merely puppets on a string was hard to swallow.

'I want you to ask them. I want to know what they think.'

Instead of giving a bellow of indignation, he chuckled.

'You're a tough one.'

'You may walk all over the men, but I'm a woman, *Grand-père*, and you're not going to walk all over me.'

Another chuckle. 'You've got spirit, anyway, and a good brain, which I already knew, of course. I think you'll do very well in Paris.'

'I haven't decided that's what I want to do.'

Living in Paris had its attractions. Taking on the responsibility of being a part of the company was a major challenge, a challenge she could get very excited about if she would let herself. She had never really thought about it, knowing the chauvinistic tendencies of her crotchety old grandfather. But she knew she could not hang out on the Ipanema beach for the rest of her life, that she needed work that would give her satisfaction and self-respect and a reason to get up in the morning. Her grandfather was offering her all that.

Then there was Enrico. She closed her eyes, feeling her anger return, and something else—something more powerful than the anger. She was in love with him, and she was falling deeper every day—well, maybe not today, but most days.

So what about their relationship? She didn't know where it was going, didn't know if there really was a future. This morning, in her anger, she had sorely doubted it. Going to Paris would mean the end of their relationship. Granted, there were many long-distance love affairs and marriages these days—London-Paris, New York-San Francisco. But Paris-Rio was beyond the realm of reality.

It was too early to know what would happen. She couldn't make a decision now.

'So when are you going to decide?' her grandfather demanded.

'I don't know. I need time.'

'How much time?'

She closed her eyes. 'Give me till spring. And I want you to talk to the others about it. I want to know what they think.'

He gave a deep sigh. 'All right, all right.'

It was a victory of sorts and she smiled into the phone. *'Merci, Grand-père.'* But she was speaking to dead air. He had already hung up.

That afternoon one big, beautiful orchid was delivered to her suite. 'See you in my kitchen tonight', the message read, and despite herself, she smiled. Enrico did have a unique kind of charm, at least if he were favourably disposed towards one. If not, watch out. She felt sorry for his enemies, or anyone who wasn't in his good graces.

She placed the orchid on the coffee table, wondering if it was meant as an apology for this morning. The card didn't actually say so. She sat down on the couch and gazed at the flower, its pale pink perfection, its delicate shape. It was difficult to stay angry. She sighed and closed her eyes briefly. 'Oh, Enrico,' she muttered, 'why are you so cold-hearted sometimes?'

When it was time to get ready, she changed into jeans and a T-shirt; she could come back and dress for dinner later. She took the lift with an elderly man in a sober suit whose face radiated disapproval. Apparently she was not supposed to be dressed casually for the cocktail hour, carrying a brown paper bag. Little do you know, buddy, she told him silently. I'm going to bake me a pie.

Enrico opened the door, wearing jeans and a T-shirt as well. She liked to see him dressed in casual clothes. He closed the door and pulled her into his arms.

'I'm glad you're not angry any more.'

She pushed against him. 'Who says I'm not angry?'

'You would have stayed away.'

'We had an appointment.'

He cocked one eyebrow. 'An appointment, is that what this is?'

'You requested my culinary services, remember?'

'I was lying.'

'Well, *I* am here to bake a pie. I . . .'

He kissed her into silence. He kissed every thought in her head into nothingness. The paper bag with the can of pumpkin slipped from her fingers and dropped to the wooden floor with a loud thump. He released her and she stared at him dazedly. 'Sorry about that.'

'Sure you are. But I get the point. All right, all right, you win. Let's bake the damned pie.'

She didn't move.

'The kitchen is this way,' he said, waving his hand.

'Why did you send me the orchid?'

'A peace offering. An apology.'

'Really?'

'Yes. I'm sorry I made you angry. I didn't mean to upset you.' He touched her cheek, smiling crookedly. 'I don't like you being angry with me,' he added on a low note. 'It's not a good feeling.'

'I know.' She took his hand. 'Apology accepted.'

Chantal had not been to his apartment before and she glanced around curiously. It was spacious and light with large windows and an ocean view. It had beautiful wood floors, which, he told her, were made from some exotic tropical hardwood from the Amazon forest. The furnishings were comfortably contemporary without the stark sleekness of his office. She was glad to see that. The kitchen was small, but a marvel of modern convenience.

Enrico put the can on the counter. 'Let's have a drink while we're at it. How about some wine? Or would you rather have a mixed drink?'

'Wine is fine.' She watched him as he opened a bottle and poured them each a glass.

'Here you go.' He lifted his glass to hers. *'A sua suade.'*

She took a sip from her wine. 'Brazilian?' she asked.

'Of course. The real thing.'

'It's good.'

'Of course it's good.'

She met his eyes. 'You were right, you know,' she said slowly. 'Dominique is spoiled and wants everything her way, and I'm not condoning what she did; infidelity is a terrible thing, but she was hurting. She really did love her husband, and he treated her . . .'

'She had a strange way of showing it.'

'He had a *mistress*! He ignored her!' She sighed, making a gesture of exasperation. 'Oh, please, let's not start this all over again. I don't want to argue with you about my sister.'

He gave a groan of relief. 'Thank you.'

She took a deep breath. 'All right, let's get going. Show me where you keep things.'

He had made sure he had all the other ingredients on hand—the spices, the cream, the eggs, but he did not own a rolling-pin which she needed to roll out the pastry.

'I can use an empty bottle,' she said, at which he poured the wine into a glass juice pitcher and handed her the bottle.

'How's that?' His eyes were laughing. 'We now do have to finish the wine, you realise that?'

'You go right ahead,' she said blandly. 'My limit is two glasses. Besides, when I'm done with this bottle, you can pour the wine back in.'

He grimaced horribly. 'All that pouring will give the wine a nervous breakdown. Wine has to be rested properly to be at its best.'

'Yeah, so I've heard.'

'And you claim to be French?'

'It's the Perrydale part of me speaking. We don't worry so much about resting our wine in Perrydale.'

Laughter danced in his eyes. 'You do surprise me sometimes, *mademoiselle*.'

She reached out and lightly touched his hand. 'You surprise me too, at times,' she said softly

He curled his fingers around hers. 'It's all a surprise, isn't it?' His face was thoughtful now, and the kitchen seemed very still.

She nodded slowly. 'Yes.'

'The way I feel about you,' he said softly, with a kind of wonder in his voice. 'The way I think about you when you're not with me.'

His words warmed her and she glanced down at their hands linked together. 'I think about you all the time,' she said, not caring now about letting him know. 'I was miserable all morning.'

The silence punctuated the words, an intimate silence that vibrated with other, unspoken feelings.

He tugged at her hand and drew her closer, caressing her lips with his own. 'I like surprises,' he murmured against her mouth. 'Life without surprises is like Christmas without pumpkin pie.'

She smiled, and he tightened his arms around her. 'I can't kiss you when you're smiling.'

'I can't bake a pumpkin pie when you're kissing me.'

'Where there's a will, there's a way.'

She laughed, which made kissing even more difficult. He let her go.

'OK, you win this one too, but I intend to kiss you silly at a more opportune moment.'

She grinned. 'Yes, please. Here, open this can.'

The moment was past—a small moment of reaching out, of sharing an intimate thought. She tucked it away in her mind as if it were a rare gift, something precious to cherish, to think about some more later, when she was alone.

It didn't take long before the pie was in the oven. He poured her another glass of wine and made her sit at the breakfast bar while he took care of the clean-up quickly and efficiently. She loved watching him, seeing his lean body move around with easy, fluid movements, the long legs outlined in the close-fitting jeans.

'It's going to take an hour before it's done,' she said. 'I should probably go to my place and change clothes and then come back here. You did promise me dinner, right?'

'I have a better idea.' He drew her up into his arms. 'How about if I show you my jacuzzi?'

'You have a jacuzzi?'

'Came with the apartment, but I hardly ever use it.'

'Why?'

'I'd rather run or go swimming. But with you, I just might like to go jacuzziing.'

'That's not a word.'

He kissed her on the nose. 'Don't be difficult.' His hands slid from her waist to her hips and drew her against him. 'Come on,' he whispered. 'I want to take your clothes off. I want to take my clothes off. I want to sit in a tub of hot water with you.' His voice was soft and seductive. He nudged her backwards, out of the kitchen and into his bedroom, where he deftly took off her T-shirt and then her bra.

'Beautiful,' he said softly, kissing one breast, then the other. Her nipples reacted instantly to the warm, moist touch of his mouth and a hot, tingling sensation raced through her body. She reached out and put her hands on the back of his head, curling her fingers into the thick hair.

'Where's the jacuzzi?' she asked unsteadily.'

'Off the bathroom.' He unzipped her jeans and slipped his hands inside, spreading his fingers out over the bare skin of her hips.

She closed her eyes and found his mouth with her own, kissing him, sliding her hands under his T-shirt to feel the warm, solid strength of his back.

Swiftly, he got both of them out of their clothes. They stood close together, naked, and she felt suddenly oddly embarrassed by his body, so fully aroused, and the look in his eyes as his gaze swept over her.

'You're trembling,' he said, drawing her close.

'I can't help it,' she murmured, her mouth touching the smooth skin of his shoulder. His body felt hot against her, yet she wasn't cold, not cold at all.

He moved her back, then laid her on the bed, leaning over her, kissing her hungrily.

'The jacuzzi, she whispered.

'Who said anything about a jacuzzi?'

'You did.' She touched the dark, curly hair on his chest, feeling his heart thudding under her hand.

'I was lying.'

'You don't have a jacuzzi?'

'Sure I do, but why would I want to be in a jacuzzi when I can be in bed with you, making love?'

'You tricked me.'

'I did. Now stop talking, woman.'

She wound her arms around his neck and sighed. 'All right.' The feel of his body against her was setting her on fire. She loved the way he touched her, the gentleness of his hands, the heat of his mouth.

'How's that?' he whispered, touching her in tender, sensitive places, making her body stir restlessly, aching with a delicious desire. She clung to him, kissing his warm, damp skin, pressing herself against him, searching, wanting, desperate now to feel him inside her.

He took his time and she marvelled at his control. Then suddenly it all ended in a frenzy of passion and they clung together as the tension broke in shimmering waves of release.

Her body went limp. Exhausted and damp with exertion, her heart pounding wildly, she lay back with her eyes closed. He kissed her softly, then shifted his weight off her. 'Mmm, wonderful,' he murmured.

She curled up against him. Sated and full of sweet languor, she dozed. She wanted to stay here in his arms for the rest of her life. She wanted to learn every secret thing about him, know all his fears and joys and pains. She wanted to love him.

I do love him, she thought, and smiled to herself, sighing with deep contentment. I do love him.

She had no idea what time it was when she suddenly jerked straight up in bed.

'The pie! Oh, damn!' She thrust her hands into her hair and glanced at the clock, then fell back on to the pillow, defeated.

He rolled off the bed with a groan. 'I'll go and turn the oven off.'

'It's too late. It's gone, burned and dead.'

'I'll still turn off the oven or we'll burn the whole place down.'

She watched as he walked from the room, stark naked, and then, despite herself, began to laugh.

He came back a moment later and dropped back on the bed.

'Pretty bad, right?' she asked.

'Best pumpkin pie I ever saw, just don't look at the black crust and the burned top. Underneath it's lovely. We can have it for breakfast.'

The day before Nelida was due to leave, Chantal took her out to lunch at her favourite Italian restaurant.

'This is so nice of you,' Nelida said. 'I'm going to miss you. Maybe you should come to visit us some time. There's more to Brazil than Rio, you know.'

Chantal nodded solemnly. 'I hear there are coffee plantations and cattle ranches and mean Indians and lots of dangerous jungles. And voodoo worshippers everywhere, let's not forget that.'

Nelida laughed. 'And everybody in the north sleeps in hammocks. That's what some people believe. And in the south everybody is a *gaucho* and races around on horseback.'

Chantal buttered a piece of warm, crusty bread. Nelida was right. If she wanted to know more about the country, sitting at Ipanema Beach, wonderful as it was, wouldn't get her anywhere. 'I would like to travel around, but this place is so huge, I wouldn't know where to start.'

'Start with Bahia. Come and see me and my family.'

'Thank you. I'll think about it.'

Nelida took another bite of her food, which silenced her, but not for long.

'You know what I've noticed?' she asked. 'Enrico seems so much happier than last time I saw him. He seems easier going. He smiles all the time.' She tilted her curly head and regarded Chantal speculatively. 'It's because of you, isn't it?'

'Why do you think that?'

There was laughter in the bright blue eyes. 'I know my big brother and I think he is very much in love with you.'

Chantal was silent, feeling a little uneasy. She twirled her fork around in the *linguini*.

'You're not saying anything.'

'I don't know what to say. I'm glad you think he's happier.'

'Oh, he is!' Nelida sighed. 'He's such a driven person. You must know that. It seems to me as if he's always searching for something. I don't know if I can explain this right, but he's never been a very happy man, despite all his success and all his money.'

'Why wasn't he happy?'

Nelida frowned. 'I think it all had to do with my father and us coming here to Brazil. He was fifteen at the time and he didn't want to come here. He was on the basketball team and he was the smartest in his class. He didn't want to leave his school and everything behind.'

'And you? Did you like coming here?'

'Oh, yes! I'm really happy here. I mean, it was difficult at first, but I just loved having all this family here. I had ten cousins and all those aunts and uncles and real grandparents and . . .' she made a vague gesture. 'I'm a family person. I like to know I belong somewhere.'

'And your family in Connecticut never helped you at all?' Chantal felt guilty mentioning it. She knew she was taking advantage of Miss Waterfall to get information. Nelida was so eager to talk, to tell all, that it was hard to resist. Chantal forced away the guilt. She had, after all, an excuse. She wanted so very much to know more about Enrico, to find out the secret depths of him, to understand him. He didn't talk much about himself, and she found it awkward asking him questions.

Shadows slipped across Nelida's face. 'They didn't want anything to do with us. My father had always been the black sheep of the family. He didn't want to be a banker. He didn't want to do anything they wanted him to do. Then he went on this trip around the world and came back with my mother. They'd already married and he'd never even told his family.

They were furious. My mother wasn't at all the kind of woman they wanted in the family. She was just an ordinary middle-class person and a foreigner at that. She didn't speak English and she didn't know how to dress and she didn't fit in at all.' She looked away. 'They cut him out of the will. He had money of his own that had come to him through his grandfather who'd already died. They couldn't touch that, of course, so we never even knew he'd been cut out. He never told us. My mother thought we were well off and we had nothing to worry about. Then my father died and everything went wrong. It was a terrible time. My mother found out that my father had gambled heavily and there was nothing left but debts, and that he'd spent thousands on . . .' She bit her lip. 'I think that finally broke her.'

'It must have been terrible.'

'I was very young. I didn't know what was going on, but Enrico did. It changed him. He became hard and cold and very driven. He hated my father. He didn't want to talk about him or even mention his name. My mother had to go out to work to keep us going. She hadn't been trained for anything, so she became a maid in a Marriott Hotel, making beds, cleaning bathrooms, you know, that sort of thing.' She stopped, her blue eyes clouded.

'Sometimes we would wait for her in the lobby, quiet as little mice so they wouldn't throw us out. We would just sit there and stare at the people coming and going, feeling like poor little nobodies. We'd had to sell our house and we lived in this dinky little apartment with hardly any furniture. There was so little money we couldn't buy new clothes, so my mother got second-hand ones for us from a church organisation.' She sighed again. 'None of this affected me so much. I was too little to realise what was going on, but my sister and Enrico were angry and upset all the time. Finally

my mother couldn't take it any more and decided to go back to
Brazil. Her father, my grandfather, took out his life savings
and paid for our tickets.' She paused. 'Getting the five of us
back to Brazil took *all* his money. And to think that minutes
away from where we lived in Connecticut we had wealthy
grandparents who never lifted a finger to help us.' She shook
her head, apparently still incredulous. 'Here, in Brazil, family
means everything.'

Enrico was busy with a reception that evening, and she didn't
see him until he came to her room late that evening. She didn't
mention anything Nelida had said. Chantal had the feeling
Enrico wouldn't like his sister telling her the family secrets.
She hoped that eventually he would trust her enough to tell
her himself. Tonight she didn't want anything to disturb the
peace. Tomorrow he and Nelida would go to Bahia to
celebrate Christmas at home. Enrico wouldn't be back for
several days. All she wanted this night was to love him.

He took her in his arms and held her close. 'You have no
idea how good it feels to come home to a warm, loving woman
after a day like this.' He kissed her. 'Or after any day at all.'

They made wonderful, passionate love and as she lay next to
him in the big bed, watching his face relaxed in sleep, her
heart swelled with the depth of her feelings for him.

So much she didn't know and understand about him, so
many secret depths she wanted to discover. She knew the
arrogant, cold exterior she had encountered on her arrival hid a
wealth of anger and pain—a father who had been a no-good
philanderer who had cheated on his wife and gambled away all
the money.

She lay on her side and gently laid her hand on his chest. He
was breathing regularly and she felt the steady beat of his heart
under her fingers. She thought of his mother, who'd

gone to work as a hotel maid. Could that possibly have anything to do with Enrico now running one of the most exclusive hotels in the world? She imagined him sitting in the lobby, waiting with his two sisters for his mother to finish work, watching the comings and goings of the guests. Was it any wonder Enrico was bitter and cold? *I don't abide women who cheat on their husbands and men who cheat on their wives.* The words he had said a few days ago, came back to her now. David's face flashed before her mind's eye, then was gone. Unfaithfulness created nothing but misery and pain.

Enrico stirred in his sleep, turning over and reaching out a hand, touching her. He mumbled something unintelligible.

'What?' she whispered.

'Don't go away,' he muttered.'

'I'm not going.' She snuggled closer to the warmth of his body, knowing there was no going back now.

She loved him more than she had ever loved anybody.

Christmas Eve was busy and exciting. Dominique and Chantal helped *Maman* get organised for the festivities. There were packages under the tree, wrapped in colourful paper and tied with ribbons and bows. The elegant apartment looked beautiful with the decorations the three of them had put up a few days ago.

'An American Christmas,' Dominique said, sipping some egg-nog Chantal had made. 'It's the best there is.' She smiled wistfully. 'I always did like coming home to you and Dad at Christmas time. You always made such a fuss.'

'I'm glad.' Chantal felt her throat close up. The sorrow was still there. This would be the first Christmas without her father and she missed him.

Dominique hugged her in a rare show of affection. 'What I would like is for us to have an American Christmas every year, wherever we are. A family tradition.'

'That would be wonderful.' Chantal smiled. 'Midnight Mass on Christmas Eve, opening presents on Christmas morning and then a turkey dinner in the afternoon.' They had already planned it for this Christmas, an intimate celebration in their mother's apartment with a home-cooked meal Chantal and Dominique were preparing in *Maman's* desperately under-used kitchen.

Chantal surveyed the room. 'Well, let's see. What else do we need here?'

Maman and Uncle Matteus arrived a few moments later and they all sat down and had cocktails before going out to dinner. Uncle Matteus was in a wonderful mood. He had finalised negotiations for the take-over of a large hotel in Madrid and he was ready to start a total renovation of the place. Extensive designs had already been prepared and an army of decorators and workmen stood at the ready to start work the first of the year.

Chantal always enjoyed talking with Uncle Matteus. He was a dynamic man who was not satisfied just sitting around and keeping things going. He needed new challenges, new territory to conquer to keep his juices flowing. His next project was already under way—plans to build a new hotel in Singapore, complete with its own shopping centre. In Singapore, he explained, you don't build a hotel without attaching a shopping centre.

Maman glanced at her watch. 'It's getting late. We'd better get changed. Chantal, *chérie*, why don't you come back here when you're ready and we'll all leave together.'

Chantal took the lift back to her suite. She opened the door and went in, her eyes catching the envelope on the silver tray on the coffee table. Maybe a message from Enrico. Quickly she opened the envelope and extracted the piece of paper.

It wasn't from Enrico.

Her heart began to pound. It was another telex from Minneapolis. '*MERRY CHRISTMAS*,' it read. '*M*'.

There was nothing else. Just that. No threat, no warning. So why then was her heart pounding?

She threw the paper back on the table and clenched her hands. 'Oh, damn!' she muttered. 'Oh, damn!'

She was determined not to let the telex spoil her Christmas, but it was difficult not to think about it. All through the rest of the evening, during Mass, and all Christmas day, her thoughts kept turning back to it. She didn't mention the telex to Dominique. There was no use in her being concerned about it as well. Besides, what was there to be concerned about? M, whoever he or she was, had merely wished her a Merry Christmas. It was what millions of people all over the world wished each other.

It was the fact she didn't know this M that bothered her. This is the last time I'm going to take it, she told herself. One more of these and I'm going to find out what's going on. Having made that decision made her feel better, although she had no idea how she would go about finding out. Enrico would knw. There had to be ways of tracing anonymous telexes.

Despite her apprehensions about the telex and the memories of her father, Christmas was a happy time. Unwrapping presents was a treat with Nicole's excitement and enthusiasm lending great cheer to the occasion. There were packages from both Nelida and Enrico for Chantal—a beautiful, artistic book of photographs of Brazil from Nelida and a gold necklace with a charm from Enrico.

'It's a *figa*,' Maman said. 'A good-luck charm. Haven't you seen them? Lots of people wear them. Plastic and wooden ones

—all kinds.'

Chantal examined the charm which lay heavily in her hand. It was a small clenched fist with a thumb protruding between the first and second finger. A good-luck charm, and Enrico had given it to her. It was a lovely present—not ostentatious or pretentious, just a simple gift of good luck.

'It's all superstition, of course,' said Dominque. 'Something to do with those strange, mixed-up religions of the black people here.'

'Enrico told me. I think it's fascinating. He's going to take me to the beach on New Year's Eve to watch the celebration.'

The turkey dinner turned out beautifully and they all enjoyed the warm family atmosphere. Uncle Matteus glanced around the table as they were all eating, smiling broadly. 'Just what I always wanted,' he said. 'A real family.'

If only Enrico could have been here. Chantal thought silently.

She was happy to see him again two days later.

'I missed you,' he said, holding her tight. 'I'm getting addicted to having you around.'

She gave him a long, lingering kiss. 'I'm glad you're back. And thank you for the *figa*.' She touched the charm. 'I'm wearing it every day. It's lovely.'

'Now you'll have good luck for ever and ever.'

She smiled. 'Yes. As long as you stay around.'

His eyes held hers. 'It's a deal.' He kissed her—a long, passionate kiss that left her breathless and warm with excitement. His hand moved under her shirt, stroking her bare back.

'They're waiting for you in the office,' she whispered.

'Let them wait. GMs are supposed to have a cool head and if I don't make love to you now, this very moment, I'll go stark, raving mad. We can't afford that, can we?'

'You mean to say you have no control over yourself?'

He slipped her shirt over her head. 'Absolutely none.' He proceeded to take off the rest of her clothes, kissing her all over, then took off his own, while he kept on kissing her.

He put her down on the floor, on the soft pale carpeting, his body trembling with impatience, his mouth hot and hungry.

'You're an animal,' she whispered. 'I like it.'

'And you are the sexiest, loveliest woman in the world.'

'Liar. That's Sophia Loren.'

'She's married.'

'That's got nothing to do with whether she is sexy and lovely or not.'

'At a time like this you expect me to be logical?'

'I suppose that's asking too much from someone with a Harvard degree?'

'Be quiet,' he whispered, closing his mouth over hers.

She had not expected the scene she witnessed on the beach on New Year's Eve. It was crowded with voodoo worshippers wearing white robes. Candles flickered everywhere amid the offerings of fresh flowers and *cachaça*, brought for Iemanjá, the goddess of the sea.

'It's a celebration of thanksgiving,' Enrico said, as they made their way through the throngs of people, careful not to step on anything. 'And the time to ask for what you want in the new year.'

People were singing. Drummers were drumming. Strange signs were drawn in the sand. There was an energy in the air, a frenzy that was a little frightening. She couldn't really say why. She had never been close to anything quite so exotically pagan. It seemed that all those candles, those strangely robed people, the chanting and dancing created an almost hypnotic atmosphere. Holding on to Enrico's hand, Chantal looked around in amazement and disbelief. 'What's that?' she asked, as they passed a white cloth with a display of cosmetics and jewellery and bottles of wine. A chain of candles surrounded the cloth and a woman in a white robe was singing over it.

'More offerings.' He sounded mildly amused. 'Iemanjá needs all these things to keep her beautiful and happy.'

'What happens with all that stuff?'

'Just you wait. You'll see when it's midnight.'

And she did see. Fireworks lit up the sky, bells began to ring, sirens wailed in a cacophony of sound. Her heart jumped with the sudden outbrust of noise. Crying, singing, shrieking, the worshippers rushed into the water in a frenzy of emotion, offering their gifts to the waves to carry them further away into the sea. Mass hysteria. She had never seen anything like it and the intensity frightened her a little.

Amid the noise and frenzy, Enrico took her face in his hands and kissed her long and hard. 'Happy New Year,' he said, gazing into her eyes with a look that made her tremble.

'Happy New Year.'

'Have you made your wishes?'

'Yes,' she whispered, fingering the gold *figa*. For you to love me always, she added silently, feeling his lips warm on hers.

And then it was over. The excitement died down. Slowly, the masses of humanity drifted away and went home.

'Now Iemanjá is happy.' Enrico's voice was low and amused. 'And everybody's wishes will be granted, at least they all hope so.' He pressed her closer, his face against her hair. 'I hope so too.'

The following weeks were sheer bliss. In his free time Enrico took her around Rio. They had a wonderful day boating in Guanabara Bay, found a small cove for swimming on Paqueta island, and had a luscious picnic prepared by the hotel.

They visited lovely old churches and one Sunday afternoon they went for a drive through the luxuriant vegetation of Tijuca National Park. At night they ate in small, intimate restaurants, avoiding the more exclusive places the elite patronised. He took her to ballet performances and concerts and one night they went to see a performance of the famous Beija-Flor samba school.

She enjoyed it all, finding Rio exciting and alive, a hedonistic, exotic paradise. Yet that was only part of this *cidade maravilhosa*, and she was well aware of it. She was appalled at the depressing squalor of the *favelas*, the shanty towns without running water or sewage that were home to thousands of people. A problem of massive proportions, Enrico told her, and she listened to him as he explained about the measures being taken to solve it.

As the weeks passed, her feelings for Enrico grew more intense. He was loving, considerate, and a wonderful lover. She knew that if her grandfather called to see about her coming to France, there was only one answer she could give him. Maybe it was foolish to throw away the opportunity of being part of the family company, yet she knew that love meant more to her than anything. Love to last a lifetime.

Sometimes, when she was alone, fear assailed her. Her mother had given up a lot when she married her father and in the end it had not worked. In the end she had gone back to the world where she had come from, where she really belonged.

And where do I belong? she asked herself. In Perrydale? In France? No. It wasn't a place that mattered. It was love and family and a shared life that was most important. That's why she had stayed with her father. That's why she was here in Rio now.

Yet something clouded her happiness. Enrico never said he loved her. She wondered about his deeper feelings, what he wanted out of life. Did he want a wife and family? Did he want marriage? He never broached the subject of marriage, not even in general. Maybe he was afraid of marriage. After all he was thirty-six and never had been married before. His mother's marriage to his father had ended in disaster. Adding it all up, maybe he simply didn't believe it could ever work.

She didn't want to worry about it, about the future and what would happen. From all evidence, it did appear that Enrico considered their relationship a long-term arrangement. She had asked him what to be prepared for and he had said, '*to take this relationship seriously. To take my feelings for you seriously.*'

I want everything too fast, she thought. Give it some time. As long as they took each other seriously, nothing else really mattered.

Chantal was ready to go down to dinner when she heard a knock on her door. In her stockinged feet she crossed the sitting-room, opened the door and froze.

Tall, blond and blue-eyed, the man regarded her silently and waited.

'*David?*' She stood stock still, staring, her heart racing. It couldn't be true. It wasn't possible. 'David?' she whispered incredulously. 'What are you doing here?'

CHAPTER EIGHT

'I'M here to see you.'

She shook her head, raising her hands as if to ward him off. 'No, oh, no! I don't believe this! This is crazy!' How had he found out what suite she was staying in? The desk hadn't called to say he was here to see her.

He stepped inside and closed it behind him. 'I told you I would come for you.'

'I told you not to! I told you I *never* wanted to see you again!'

He winced. 'You also told me you loved me.'

Anger washed over her. 'You weren't the person I thought you were,' she said coldly. 'I was stupid and naïve and I would like you to leave now. I'm getting ready to go out and I need to finish dressing.' She was having dinner with her mother and Uncle Matteus and several of their friends to celebrate Uncle Matteus's birthday.

Pain flashed in his eyes and for a moment he was silent. 'I know I misled you,' he said softly, 'but I want to start over again and do it right.'

She shook her head. 'It's too late.' She reached for the door to open it, but he grasped her wrist and stopped her. He pulled her closer, looking down at her. 'I'm a free man now,' he said quietly.

She glared at him, wrenching her hands free. 'I hope it wasn't too much trouble dumping your wife!'

His face turned pale. 'It was the most difficult thing I've ever had to do.'

'Well, don't come to me for sympathy.'

'I don't want your sympathy. I want your love.'

'You don't get that on demand, David. I'm sorry, but it's over.' She looked at him and felt nothing. No love. Not even anger or bitterness. He was as handsome as ever—tall and blond with blue eyes and a boyish grin. Only the grin was not there now and the blue eyes were cloudy. She had once loved this man, or at least she had thought she had, but there was nothing left of it now.

'All I want is for you to listen to me,' he said. 'You have to say nothing, do nothing, promise nothing. Just listen to me. Please.'

'Why? It won't make any difference.'

'It will make a difference to me. I want you to know. I want you to understand.' Hi eyes were weary and she noticed the deep lines of fatigue running next to his mouth.

'Is that why you came all the way to Brazil? Just to talk to me?'

He closed his eyes briefly. 'No. But if you'll just listen to me, if you'll just let me explain . . .'

Listen. She was supposed to be a good listener. People always told her that. She sighed wearily. She didn't want to listen now. Not to David. She had listened to Dominique and the miseries of her life. She had listened to Nelida and the stories of Enrico's past. Granted, she had invited them; she had wanted to know. They were all connected to Enciro. But David was history. She didn't want to hear the tragedies of his failed marriage. It had nothing to do with her any more. She didn't want to listen to one more tale of woe.

'Please,' he said softly. 'All I want is an hour of your time.'

An hour. One hour. 'And then what?'

There was a silence and she knew he was fighting with himself. 'Then I will go back home if that's what you want.'

But he hoped she wouldn't want him to. It was obvious

enough he hadn't given up hope. He must still want her badly
if he had come all the way to Rio. She felt helpless. She didn't
want to give him any hope, but she felt almost sorry for him
now with that pleading look in his blue eyes. What was left of
this determined, self-assured commodity-broker she had once
known? This was not the man she remembered.

She squared her shoulders and met his eyes. 'All right,
David,' she said in a cool, businesslike tone, 'If it means that
much to you, I'll listen, but not now. I'm on my way out.
What about tomorrow at seven in the cocktail bar downstairs?
The one off the lobby.' She didn't want to talk here, in her
suite, and be alone with him. She didn't want him to get any
ideas. A public place was better under the circumstances.

He raked his fingers through his neatly trimmed hair. 'I'll be
there.'

He left and she closed the door behind him. She slumped
into a chair, suddenly bone weary. Why did David have to
show up now? She didn't need this. In her mind and heart she
had dealt with David; she didn't want him back in her life. She
didn't want to deal with him all over again.

Yet he was here and she had promised to listen to him.

And then he'll leave, she said to herself.

Twenty guests had gathered in one of the private dining-rooms
of the hotel. Enrico was there as well as Dominique, who sat at
the other end of the table. Dominique ignored Enrico, but it
wasn't really noticeable to anyone but Chantal. Dominique
seemed to have accepted the fact that Chantal was in love with
Enrico. She no longer said anything about it and Chantal was
glad. At least it had not caused a rift between them. The last
thing she had said was that she hoped her sister was prepared
for the inevitable end. 'With a man like Enrico it's never going
to last, you do realise that, don't you?'

'Don't worry about me, Dominique.'

'You're my sister, and I *am* worried about you!'

'I can take care of myself.'

Dominique had sighed and raised her hands in an expression of helplessness. 'Don't say I didn't warn you.'

It was a very enjoyable meal and afterwards Chantal and Enrico took a walk along the beach and talked, holding hands. It was such a simple little thing, holding hands, yet it gave her such a deep sense of closeness and intimacy.

She let out a deep sigh of contentment. She loved the smell of the sea air, the sound of the waves, the dark night sky stretched endlessly above. It made her feel close to nature, close to the man next to her. Everything felt right and good between them and love washed over her like a warm wave. She stopped walking and turned to him, smiling up at him. She put her arms around him and kissed him with a rush of passion.

I love you, she wanted to say, but kept the words inside. I love you, please tell me you love me too.

He returned her kisses with a passion of his own, holding her close against him. Then slowly they walked back to the Palácio and up to her suite.

They made love with warmth and tenderness and passion. She felt the love in his touch, saw it in his eyes, yet he didn't speak the words.

I love you, she said silently, please tell me you love me too.

She wanted to hear him say it, feeling ungrateful when she couldn't help but feel the disappointment. Wasn't it clear he loved her? Why couldn't she accept the silent love he offered her? For many men it was so hard to express their feelings, and certainly for a man like Enrico.

Maybe she was expecting too much too soon.

It will come, she thought. It will come.

*   *   *

The next morning the phone awakened her. She reached for the receiver, hearing Enrico's muttered curse as he turned over next to her in bed.

It was her grandfather calling from Paris. She gave an exasperated sigh. '*Grand-père*, it's five-thirty in the morning!'

'Well, it isn't here and I've been up for hours.'

'You woke me up,' she said with mild accusation.

'You shouldn't be sleeping the day away, or you'll never get anywhere.'

There was no getting an apology out of the old man, so she gave up trying. 'All right, what is it?'

'I wanted to let you know I spoke to your uncle and cousins about your joining the company.' He talked as if her coming to Paris was a *fait accompli*.

'And what did they say?'

'They said there is plenty of room for you and that as long as you perform the way you're expected to perform they have no objections.'

'Is that what they really think or is that what you told them to think?'

'He chuckled. 'They always think what I tell 'em to think.'

She felt Enrico's hand on her stomach, warm and sensuous. 'You are the worst manipulator I have ever known.'

'How else am I supposed to make this business run, little girl?'

'How about fair dealings, honesty, and trusting in other people's capabilities.'

'You have a lot to learn but not to worry. I'll teach you myself.'

'*Grand-père*, you promised me I had until spring to decide. Don't push me.'

'I'm not pushing you.'

'Yes you are. And I really think it's not going to work. I

would like to take the job, well, maybe, but I don't want to leave here.' She paused, glancing over at Enrico, who lay on his side, eyes open, watching her. 'I've met a man.'

'A man? Humpf! What does he do?'

'He's a hotel manager.'

'A hotel manager? *Mon Dieu*! Couldn't you do better than that?'

It should have made her angry, yet it was impossible to be angry with her grandfather. She met Enrico's eyes and grinned.

'He can manage a hotel here. Lots of hotels here. I can fix it. Is he any good?'

Chantal laughed. The very idea of her grandfather taking charge of Enrico's career was a joke. 'Very.'

'Leave it to me.'

'You might want to reconsider this, *Grand-père*. We're not talking about just any manager. We're talking about the General Manager of the Palácio Hotel.'

'Matteus's boy?'

She eyed Enrico's bare chest, wide and brown and covered with dark curly hair and bit her lip. 'Yes, Matteus's boy.'

Enrico's brows rose at that and her eyes laughed into his.

Her grandfather snorted with frustration. 'Well, you sure made a mess of that, didn't you?'

'I did? Oh, I don't think so, *Grand-père*.' She felt Enrico's hand trailing from her stomach to her breast. 'He's pretty good to me.'

'I damn well hope so!' He crashed down the receiver and Chantal winced. Oh, boy, she thought, now he's angry. He doesn't like losing.

'What job?' Enrico asked, nuzzling her neck.

'I'm not sure. He wants me to join the family company, but he's a male chauvinist of the worst sort. He'll have me licking stamps, probably.'

'Why would he want you to do that?'

'Mostly because he wants me in France, close by so that he can keep an eye on me. He doesn't want anybody else in the family marrying a Brazilian and going off to live with the injuns.'

He grinned. 'Yeah, I can see his problem.' He turned over and pulled her into his arms. 'So you don't want to live in Paris?'

'I like Rio better.'

'Why is that?'

'Because you're here, that's why.'

'And you're going to give up running the family company for me?'

'I won't be running the family company and even so I wouldn't be giving it up for you. Don't you go gettin' any ideas, *senhor*. I'd be giving it up for myself.'

'You're very clever. Don't want me to feel guilty over holding you back, do you?'

'Nobody holds me back. I'm responsible for myself. I made my own decision, and deciding not to work for that grouchy old chauvinist is probably the best one I've ever made.'

'OK, OK, I give.' He kissed her lazily.

She wriggled against him. 'Besides, if he really wants me in the company and I refuse to come to Paris he'll think of something else.'

'Like what?'

'He'll get something going here in Rio. Buy a business and get me involved. A couple of hotels of something.' She grinned. 'Maybe he'll buy the Palácio off Uncle Matteus, fire you and make me the GM.'

'Hah!' He tickled her in the ribs and she squirmed under him.

'Stop it!'

'Take it back.'

'Oh, don't worry. I'll hire you back. You can be my assistant.'

He shook his head. 'No good. If you want to be a GM, get your own hotel.'

'All right, all right, if you're going to be like that about it. I'll tell my grandfather to buy me my own hotel.'

He nuzzled her neck. 'That's the spirit.'

His bare body felt warm against her. She stroked the smooth skin of his back, feeling desire stir inside her. She closed her eyes and sighed. He kissed her neck, her chin, her cheek.

'Well,' he said in her ear, 'as long as we are awake, we might as well make love.'

'Yeah, sure,' she whispered back. 'I've got nothing better to do. What about you?'

He drew her very close. 'Nothing, nothing better, ever.'

Chantal put on a simple white dress for her meeting with David that evening. Nothing suggestive, nothing too inviting, she had decided. She examined herself in the mirror. She looked cool and collected. She didn't feel cool and collected. She wished the whole ordeal were over with.

He was already there when she arrived, sitting at one of the low tables with a view of the fountain in the lobby.

'Hello, Chantal.' His eyes slid over her with admiration. 'You look beautiful.'

'Thank you,' she said evenly. She sat down in the deep, upholstered chair opposite him. The chairs were as comfortable as any she had ever sat in, inviting a long spell of sitting and sipping of cocktails.

'This is quite a place,' he said, gesturing at the fountain and the luxurious lobby with its marble floors and exquisite tapestries.

'Yes.'

'Your stepfather owns it?'

She nodded. 'And a few others around the world.'

'Lucky man.' He beckoned the waiter, who came over immediately to take their orders.

'I'll have some dry white wine. Domestic, please.'

David frowned. 'Brazilian wine? Is it any good?' He looked dubious. He prided himself on being something of a wine connoisseur. When they went out to dinner in Chicago, he had always been careful in selecting just the right wine to go with their meal.

'Quite good, yes, or I wouldn't order it.'

'No, of course not.' He turned to the waiter, who stood by patiently. 'I'll have Scotch on the rocks, please. Glenfiddich, if you have it.'

'Yes, sir.' The waiter disppeared. It took only moments before he was back with their drinks and a dish of mixed nuts.

They sipped their drinks in silence.

'Where are you staying? Here?' Chantal asked at last.

He laughed. It was a dry humourless laugh, not at all the one she was used to from David. He shook his head. 'No, I'm in a small place at the Copacabana. I can't afford a palace. Business has not been good lately and I have Amanda's bills to pay.'

'I thought you said you were divorced.'

'Paying Amanda's bills is part of the settlement package.' He grimaced. 'She's in therapy. She's been in therapy for years. She's a very unhappy, unstable person.'

Chantal said nothing. She gritted her teeth. Now she was going to hear all about how his wife was an awful, selfish witch who did not understand him.

'I never knew how to tell you about Amanda,' he said helplessly.

'You didn't have to tell me anything. All you needed to tell me was that you were married.

'And then what?'

'Then nothing! I don't take away other women's husbands! You made me do something I always said I would *never* do! I do *not* get involved with married men!'

'You didn't take me away from her, Chantal. In every real sense I was long gone.' He swallowed visibly. 'And then you came into my life. I needed you. I needed you desperately. I couldn't take the risk of losing you.'

'So you lied to me deliberately. You misled me and you deceived me for over a year! And what about your wife? Why was she unhappy and unstable? Maybe she needed you and you weren't there for her.'

There was a silence. Chantal fought to keep her cool. Don't let him think you still care, she told herself. No sense in getting all worked up over it now.'

'Chantal, our marriage was wrong from the beginning. It was a terrrible mistake and we're both paying for it. I'll take part of the blame, but not all.'

'Then why didn't you get a divorce sooner? Why wait all this time?'

'I was afraid for Amanda. I thought she would go under. I was hoping she would pull herself together eventually, but it only got worse. I am not responsible for Amanda's problems and I dealt with them as long as I possibly could.'

Chantal gave him a scathing look. 'Until I found out that you were married. Then suddenly you decided to do something about it.'

'I knew I had to make a decision, and I did. I know I'd been putting it off and putting it off. The first time I mentioned a divorce to her, before I met you, she became hysterical.' He paused. 'She is a clinger. She wanted to hang on despite the fact that were was nothing left to hang on to.'

Chantal listened. She didn't want to hear all the miseries of his married life, but she listened. She made no further comment, but sat silently sipping her wine. The waiter came by and poured her another. David went on talking. He talked for more than an hour, drinking two more whiskys.

The piano player had arrived and music softly, discreetly undulated through the air.

She wanted to leave. She wanted to hear no more. But David did not stop. He went on, dragging up more unhappiness with each new drink. It became increasingly clear that David had not dealt with his problems well, had shown a great lack of strength and courage. Apparently, his courage was reserved for his work as a commodity-broker only.

'I needed you,' he said at last, with the helpless of despair in his voice. 'Do you understand?'

'Yes.' She did understand, but one thing remained unchanged: despite all his problems, he had not had the right to use her the way he had. He had lost her respect and killed her love.

He stopped talking, staring silently into his empty glass. She hoped he would not order another one. Finally he lifted his face, his eyes dull.

'You don't love me any more, do you?'

She shook her head, feeling compassion, but no regret. 'I'm sorry, David.'

'I did this all wrong, didn't I? I did everything wrong.'

'You can start over again. It's never too late for that.'

'I wanted to start over again with you.'

She shook her head. 'It can't be me. You can't build a relationship on a lie, David. Maybe there'll be somebody else.' She came slowly to her feet. 'Goodbye, David. I wish you happiness, truly.'

She left him in the bar and made her way back up to her suite. She felt wrung out, but she knew she didn't want to spend the rest of the evening alone to hash over David's story in her mind. She wanted to forget it, fast. She called Dominique.

It took a long time for Dominique to answer her phone and Chantal was just about to hang up when she finally came on the phone, a little breathless.

'Dominique? I thought you weren't home.'

'I was in the shower. What's up?'

Chantal took a deep breath. 'David is here.'

'*David*?'

'Yes. I just spent two hours listening to him talk. He got a divorce.'

'Oh, *bon Dieu*! And now he wants you back.'

'Yes, but I told him it was no use. I think he understands that.' She sighed. 'What are you doing tonight? Enrico is wining and dining some VIPs from England and I don't feel like sitting around by myself.'

'Bernard and I are going to a party. Why don't you join us?'

'Are you sure?'

'Positive. It's at the French Embassy. Probably not too exciting, but we'll go somewhere more interesting afterwards.'

'I'd like to come, if Bernard doesn't mind.'

Dominique laughed. 'If I'm happy, he's happy.'

Chantal couldn't suppress a smile. So with Bernard Dominique got her way too.

'We'll pick you up in about an hour, all right?'

As Dominique had predicted, the party at the French Embassy wasn't terribly exciting, but it did manage to take her mind off David. Afterwards, they went with several of Bernard's friends to a night-club where an excellent band played the most wonderful Brazilian jazz. She enjoyed the music and the conversation, which centered on politics and the preparations for the upcoming carnival. She was looking forward to the festivities, and the lavish costume ball the Palácio was organising.

It was almost three when she finally made it back to her rooms and after a quick shower, she fell into bed and was asleep almost immediately.

When she finally woke up, she was still tired. Peering at the clock with one eye, she turned over and closed her eyes again. She was too late to meet Enrico at the beach this morning; he would have to forgive her.

She had barely gone back to sleep when the phone rang and she groaned as she groped for the receiver.

'Hello?'

'Chantal?' It was Enrico, his voice strangely curt.

'I'm sorry I didn't make it to the beach this morning,' she said, 'but I overslept.'

'I'm coming up to see you.'

'I'm tired. Be nice and just let me sleep.'

'I'll be right there.' The phone went dead.

She sighed and put the receiver down. What was the matter with him? Was he mad because she didn't show up at the beach this morning? Through the crack in the curtains she could see the bright sunlight outside. It would be blistering hot already probably, but it felt nice and cool inside her room. She pulled the covers back over her head and closed her eyes.

A few minutes later a knock on the door announced Enrico's arrival. She dragged herself out of bed, struggled her bare body into a robe and opened the door for him.

He was dressed in his black suit and his hair was still damp from the shower. She stood on tiptoe and kissed his cheek, freshly shaved and smelling of aftershave.

'I'm sorry I made you wait. Are you mad at me?'

'Where were you all night?'

She stared at him. 'Where was I all night? Here, in bed, of course.' She pointed at the bed through the open double doors. 'What's the matter?'

'You weren't there at twleve, nor at one, nor at two.'

She felt suddenly cold. She didn't like the tone of his voice.

'I went out,' she said quietly. 'I came home just before three.'

'You told me you were going to stay home. Watch a movie.' His voice was cold and accusing.

'I changed my mind.' He had told her not to expect him that evening. Entertaining the Lord and Lady would probably take some time and she shouldn't wait up for him.

'So where did you go? And with whom?'

Anger silenced her, but only for a moment. 'Enrico, are you asking me to account for my whereabouts? Do I need your consent to go out?' She couldn't believe what she was seeing: Enrico—suspicious, possessive, jealous. She didn't like it. She didn't like it one bit.

'Who is that man you were sitting in the bar with last night?' he demanded, not answering her question.

She closed her eyes briefly. 'So that 's what this is all about.' She turned and sank down in a chair with a deep sigh.

'Who is he?' His face was tense with strain, his eyes oddly expressionless as if he were trying to keep his emotions in, force everything behind an impenetrable wall of iron self-control. There was more than anger there, she realised, more than plain jealousy. He was afraid.

'A man I used to know in Illinois.'

'A man you used to know,' he repeated. 'What is he doing here? He's not a guest at the Palácio. I checked.

'You checked?' She stiffened and her hands clenched into fists. 'Why did you check? Can't I talk to another person without you having to check up on him?'

His jaw stiffened. 'I happened to see you in the bar with him. He was holding your hand! I wanted to know what was going on. What is he doing here, in Brazil?'

'He came to see me.' She took a steadying breath. 'And please don't question me, Enrico. This is a private, personal matter that has nothing to do with you or us.'

It wasn't that there was anything to hide, anything she didn't want him to know. One day she would most likely tell him about David, but not because he demanded an explanation.

'Like hell it doesn't!' His eyes leaped with fire. 'Last night you sat in the bar for *two hours* with a strange man, talking, drinking, and I'm not supposed to wonder? Then I come back early because Lady Whatshername gets a headache and so I call you and you're not in your room as you said you would be. You're not there at twelve and I keep calling and you're still not a home at two-thirty, but I can't ask you what this is all about?'

'I was dealing with some unfinished business, tying up some loose ends in my life.'

'Is he in love with you?'

She had dreaded the question, knowing it was coming. No man followed a woman thousands of miles to another continent without arousing suspicions of romantic involvements. 'Yes.'

'And how he's here to get you back?'

She didn't answer.

'Is he?'

She nodded. 'Yes.'

'Did you sleep with him?'

It was not anger she felt now, just a helpless despair, a pain so great it brought tears to her eyes. Slowly she got out of the chair and looked at him squarely.

'If you feel there is a need to ask that kind of a question, Enrico, then I want you to leave.' She hugged her arms to her chest. 'If you trust me so little, then . . . then there's no point in us going on.' Her voice broke and tears spilled out on to her cheeks. She turned her back to him, hunching her shoulders against the pain. 'Just get out of here, Enrico.'

No sound came from behind her, no door opening and closing. Then she felt his hands on her shoulders and she whirled around in sudden fury and faced him.

'Don't touch me!' Something broke inside her and a wildness came over her. 'How dare you? How *dare* you come in here and question me like that? How *dare* you ask me if I slept with another man?' Tears streamed down her face. Enrico was nothing but a blur and she wiped at her eyes impatiently.

'I don't *want* him back! I don't love him! And all we did last night was talk. I left him in the bar and then I went out with Dominique and Bernard, and you can check it out if you find that necessary! We went to a party at the French Embassy, then to that jazz place on Rua Rainha Elizabeth.' She took a shuddering breath. 'Go! Go on and check that out!' She swept past him, into the bedroom, and closed the door, then flung herself on to the bed and buried her face in the pillow. A storm of weeping overtook her.

There was an impatient knocking on the door but she ignored it. He could stand there all day and she wouldn't let him in.

'Chantal, let me in!'

'Go away!'

There was an horrendous noise, the splintering of wood, and she sat bolt upright in the bed. The double doors were wide open and Enrico stood at the end of her bed. She stared at him incredulously.

'You broke the doors! Are you crazy?'

'I must be,' he admitted. 'Crazy and jealous and stupid.'

She hugged her knees to her chest. She wanted to tell him to go away, but it would be a waste of breath.

He sat down on the bed, but didn't touch her. He seemed suddenly very tired and he raked his fingers through her hair with an oddly defeated gesture. 'I'm sorry, Chantal. I don't know what came over me.' He sighed heavily. 'I was up half the night wondering where you were. All I could see was this guy and the two of you holding hands.'

'We weren't holding hands. He took my hand and I pulled it back. I didn't want him holding my hand.'

There was a silence then as he watched her, his face tense with the effort to hide his emotions and she knew that something else needed to be said, but she didn't know if she dared, if she could take the risk.

You have to, a little voice said, Be the first, open up.

She moistened her dry lips. 'Enrico,' she said softly, 'it's you I love.'

A muscle jerked in his cheek, the mask crumbled and then she was in his arms and he pressed her hard against him. 'Oh, God, Chantal, I love you too, I love you too. I'm sorry I'm such a jealous bastard, but I had to know.' His mouth found hers and he kissed her wildly, hungrily.

Joy soared through her. He loved her. He had said so, finally. And all the anger and pain were fogotten. It didn't matter any more, not now. He loved her. He loved her.

She clung to him, kissing him back, and his hands slipped inside her robe and caressed her bare skin underneath.

'I was going crazy last night,' he muttered. 'All I could see was that tall blond guy and you. All night I kept making up scenarios. Oh, God, don't do that to me ever again.'

'I didn't do it to you. You did it to yourself.'

He groaned and pressed her closer against him. 'Whatever. Just tell me again you love me.'

'I love you.'

'And I love you.' His mouth searched for hers. 'I love you,' he whispered against her lips. 'I love you.'

Her happiness lasted two days.

Coming home from shopping with her mother, she found another telex waiting for her in her room, neatly displayed on the small silver tray, like an offering.

Another message from M in Minneapolis.

CHAPTER NINE

THE paper trembled in her hands. 'I SHOULD HAVE KNOWN YOU DIDN'T CARE. YOU RUINED MY LIFE. I MIGHT AS WELL BE DEAD AND IT'S ALL YOUR FAULT.'

Her heart pounded in her chest and her legs shook.

There was a knock on the door and she crossed the room to open it. It was Enrico, which surprised her. He didn't usually visit her suite in the middle of a working-day. He stepped inside and closed the door behind him. He nodded at the paper in her hand.

'I think it's time we found out who is sending you these messages.'

She stared at him. 'What do you know about this?'

He shrugged. 'After the last one I gave orders to the telex operator that I wanted to know about any telexes coming in for you.'

She was too upset to complain about his invasion of her privacy; to suggest he had no business meddling in her affairs. 'The last one? You weren't here when it came. It was the day before Christmas.'

He frowned. 'I wasn't told about that one. And you didn't mention it either.'

'It said "Merry Christmas", that's all.' She shrugged. 'I felt stupid making a fuss over an innocuous message like that.'

He took the paper from her nerveless fingers and glanced at it. 'Well, this is no innocuous message.'

She ran her tongue over her dry lips. 'What can we do?'

'Trace it. See who sent it. With your permission, of course.'

She nodded. 'All right. Please.'

She shook her head numbly.

He folded the telex and slipped it into the pocket of his jacket. Then he took her in his arms and held her quietly for a moment. 'Don't worry, we'll figure this out.' He kissed her forehead. 'Come one, let's find a cup of coffee.'

It was a matter of a few days only. Enrico came to see her again in the middle if the day, just after she had come back to her suite from a session with her Portuguese instructor. Enrico looked angry and dangerous and fear shot through her. She closed the door behind him and studied his face.

'What's wrong?'

He tapped the blue folder he held in his hand. 'I found out who sent you those telexes.'

Slowly she sat down in a chair, her heart pounding. 'Who?'

'Does the name Mandy mean anything to you?'

'Mandy?' She shooke her head. 'I don't know any Mandy.'

'How about Amanda Henredon? As in Mrs David Henredon.'

The blood drained from her face. 'Oh, my God,' she whispered, closing her eyes for a moment.

He laughed grimly. 'Ah, bingo!' He tossed the folder on the coffee-table, turned on his heel and strode out of the door.

She stared at the closed door, numb with shock. David's wife had sent her those telexes, a woman she had never met, a woman whose name she hadn't known until a few days ago when David mentioned it.

A woman whose husband she had loved for a year.

She huddled in the chair and pressed her hands against her eyes. Amanda Henredon.

'YOU RUINED MY LIFE.' Had she unwittingly done

that?

But I didn't know! I never intended any of this!

She took a deep breath and sat up straight. I am not responsible, she thought fiercely. I did nothing wrong. She took a deep steadying breath. What had David told her about Amanda? *She's a very unhappy, unstable person. She's been in therapy for years.*

Well, I had nothing to do with that, Chantal thought.

But David got a divorce from her so that he could marry you, a little voice said. Well, she certainly had not encouraged that. As soon as she had found out David had lied to her, she had broken up with him.

It was all David's fault. David who had been too weak to take charge of his life in a positive way. And he had dragged her, Chantal, into the middle of it. Now his ex-wife blamed her, and sent her disturbing messages, frightening her. Anger at David suddenly flared, but only briefly. It didn't matter any more.

It was over now. She knew who had sent her the telexes and she felt no longer afraid or threatened. She sighed. She didn't know this Amanda, but it was obvious that she was not doing well. She felt no anger towards the woman, only pity.

She picked up the folder on the table and glanced at the sheets of paper inside. It was a report from a private investigator. Apparently the case had not been a complicated one. The telex had been traced to a large export company in Minneapolis and straight to the telex operator herself, Amanda Henredon, recently divorced from David Henredon. Mr David Henredon had had a year-long relationship with a Ms Chantal Stevenson, who presently resided in Rio de Janeiro, Brazil and was the recipient of the telex in question. According to Amanda Henredon, David Henredon had divorced her so that he could marry Ms Chantal Stevenson.

She leaned back in her chair, her heart heavy.

She saw again Enrico's angry face, heard the caustic note in his voice. There was no need to ask why he had been so furious. The reason was there, in her hand. She, Chantal, had had an affair with a married man, caused the break-up of the marriage and had driven the wife to the brink of a nervous breakdown. As far as Enrico was concerned there was nothing more to be said.

Only there was so much more to be said, so much to explain.

He would have to listen to her. He loved her. Certainly once he had cooled down he would be willing to listen to reason?

Fear clutched at her heart. What if he didn't?

Of course he will! she said to herself. Of course he will! She would talk to him tonight, after the cocktail party at her mother's and Uncle Matteus's apartment.

Everything would be all right. It had to be.

He came late to the party and as she made meaningless chitchat with the various guests, her nerves were strung taut. When finally he arrived, he ignored her completely. He avoided her for more than an hour, never met her eyes and did not speak to her. To him she wasn't there. Her stomach cramped with anxiety. She felt sick.

He would never listen. He would not believe her. She closed her eyes and the pain was sharp, bringing tears to her eyes. Enrico had judged her already, not having heard a word of her defence.

I don't have to defend myself. I'm not guilty!

I'm not guilty, not guilty . . .

She searched the room with her eyes, finding him staring out of the window with a drink in his hand. Then she saw him move over to the french doors leading out on to the roof terrace and slip outside.

The party was contained inside, where the air-conditioning kept the place cool and comfortable. The sweltering January heat lay heavily over the city even at this late hour. The terrace doors were closed and no one else had ventured outside.

Swiftly, Chantal crossed the room and followed Enrico out, closing the door very quietly behind her. The air felt hot and humid, clinging around her like a wet blanket.

Enrico stood by the railing staring out of the city, glittering in the night, one hand in his pocket, the other holding the glass. She moved over and stood next to him, seeing his body tense. He said nothing, didn't look at her, but she knew he was aware of her presence.

The tension vibrated between them and Chantal felt the wild throbbing of her heart. She had to do something, say something. Most of all she had to stay calm. She fought for composure.

'I know what you're thinking,' she said quietly.

'You have no idea what I'm thinking!' his voice shot out in the silence and she winced at the viciousness in his tone.

'I never knew he was married, Enrico. I had nothing to do with his divorce.'

'You had nothing to do with his divorce?' His voice was cold with contempt. 'How else could he marry you?'

'I never knew he was married in the first place.'

'You knew him for a *year* and you didn't know he was married? My God, how stupid do you think I am? How can you possibly not know? How naïve and gullible can you possibly be?'

'Apparently enough to be fooled completely,' she said bitterly.

'You're an intelligent woman, Ms Stevenson. Don't pretend otherwise.'

Anger overwhelmed her despair. 'If I was so eager to marry

David, why did I come here?'

His smile was not friendly. 'Put on the pressure a little, perhaps? And it worked, didn't it? That besotted fool came all the way to Brazil to claim you. Only in the meantime you'd changed your mind, so you sent him packing.'

'You're despicable!'

He turned towards her so swiftly she had no chance to move away. His hands clamped around her wrists. 'You've got that wrong, sweetheart,' he said with quiet venom. 'It's *you* who's despicable.'

He tossed her hands away from him as if he could not bear to touch her any more. He opened the door and went inside, leaving her alone on the terrace in the sweltering night.

She didn't know she could feel such fury and such pain at the same time. She was trembling with it. She leaned against the railing, pressing her eyes closed, fighting for enough composure to go back in and make her way, through the happy, drinking crowd, to the front door.

Somehow she managed to escape unnoticed. She sat on the bed in her room, trembling. Seeing the contempt in Enrico's face had shaken her to the core. She kept hearing his voice, his words echoing in her mind. *It's you who's despicable!* She hugged herself and moaned.

During the next two days there was not a word of a sign from Enrico. Two days was enough, she decided. Two days was more than she could bear. Obviously he was not going to change his mind and ask for her side of the story. She would make one attempt to give it to him, but only one.

The princess wore emeralds that day, and the same haughty smile, as she showed Chantal into Enrico's office.

'What can I do for you?' he asked with frigid politeness as she stood before the huge Victorian desk.

Her heart was pounding wildly, but she faced him squarely.

'I wonder if you could spare a little time and go for a walk with me, or go some other place where we can be alone.'

'We're alone here.' His tone was uncompromising.

She wasn't going to argue with him. She sat down in a chair. 'All right, here it is.'

He glanced at his watch. 'I have a meeting in five minutes,' he said coolly. 'I'm afraid I can't spare much time.'

A bitter pain filled her and she was tempted to leave right then and there, but she knew that pride would not get her anywhere now, so she swallowd hard and held his gaze for a long, tense moment. 'I'm sorry I'm disturbing you,' she said quietly. 'I just hoped you might want to listen to my side of the story.'

'I know all I need to know.'

She suppressed her anger with an effort. 'No, you don't, Enrico.'

Steely eyes bored into hers. 'I know that there is a woman with a nervous breakdown because you were having an affair with her husband and he divorced her so that he could marry you.'

Involuntarily she flinched. It sounded so cold and cruel and heartless and it was all he saw, all he could see. His face was closed, expressionless. All the barriers were neatly in place. She would not be able to get through to him; he would hear no reason. He had already decided and found her guilty.

The irony of the situation did not escape her. She was always the listener, but now that she wanted to talk, the man she loved refused to listen. Despair filled her. She loved this man and he was beyond her reach now. She came to her feet and faced him squarely. 'Enrico, please listen to me. I didn't know he was married. *I didn't know!*'

His mouth turned down in contempt. 'And do you expect me to believe that?'

She stared at him with bitter anger, then shook her head. 'No, I don't,' she said slowly. 'I only expect the people who know and love me to believe and trust me.' She turned and rushed out of the room, away from him.

She was sitting on the bed, her face swollen, her eyes red from crying, when Dominique found her later that day.

'*Mon Dieu!* What has happened to you!' She stared at Chantal, blue eyes wide with concern.

'You were right, you know,' Chantal said bitterly. 'It couldn't last. It's over.'

Dominque sank into a chair near the bed with no pretense of elegance. 'The bastard!' she said viciously. 'What did he do to you?'

Chantal took a tissue and blew her nose. 'We discovered who has been sending me the telexes and he didn't like what he found out.' She told Dominique the story in as few words as possible. Her voice was shaky and the words came with difficulty. 'He doesn't believe I didn't know he was married.'

Dominique sighed. 'It *is* hard to believe, Chantal, I'll grant him that.' She scrutinised Chantal's face. 'Weren't there any signs at all he had a family? What about his phone number? Where did you call him?'

Chantal rubbed her face. She felt so weary and desolate. 'At home, or at his office.'

'Did you ever go home with him?'

'Of course I did. He has an apartment in Chicago. It's small, but very nice and very much a man's place. No woman lived there, or I would have noticed.'

'What about the weekends and holidays?'

'We spent a lot of weekends together. Last Christmas he went to Buffalo to be with his parents.'

'Did he ask you to come with him?'

'No. I'd asked him to spend it with us, but he couldn't, he said.'

'And he never *said* anything that gave him away? Nothing that made you wonder?'

'No.' She bit her lip. 'I never had any idea. I met his friends. We went out together, we were invited together. Nobody ever said anything about a wife. He told me, when he was here, that they had a house in Minneapolis, but he was hardly ever there. I never knew about it.'

'And when you told Enrico, he didn't believe you?'

'I didn't tell him anything. He didn't want to listen to me. All he needed to judge me was that report from the investigator.'

'He didn't even want to listen to your explanation?'

'No.'

'The self-righteous bastard!' Dominique jumped to her feet. 'God, I can't stand that man! I'm getting a drink.' She stormed over to the bar in the sitting-room and opened the refrigerator. 'You want something?' she called.

'I'll have some rum and orange juice, not too strong.'

Through the open bedroom doors, Chantal watched Dominque pour the drinks and carry them back into the bedroom. She handed Chantal a glass and sat down again in the chair.

'So now you're the wanton female who stole another woman's husband.'

Chantal winced. 'I suppose so.'

Dominique took a gulp from her drink and gave a dry little laugh. 'That fateful evening in his bedroom, he told me he finds nothing more despicable than a married woman cheating on her husband, or a husband cheating on his wife.' She took another drink. 'I expect we may safely assume he finds it equally despicable when a woman steals another woman's husband, or a man steals another man's wife.' She grimaced. 'Welcome to the club, *chérie*. Now we're both in the big, bad book. The two Wicked Sisters. Shame, shame.'

Chantal stared into her drink. *Despicable*. It was only a word, yet it had a terrible power to hurt. Again Enrico's voice echoed in her mind. *It's you who's despicable.*

Dominique stirred restlessly in her chair, as if she had a hard time controlling her anger. 'The arrogance of the man is phenomenal. Who the hell does he think he is, passing judgement?'

Chantal said nothing. She felt numb, as she had felt numb for the past two days. She sipped her drink. One thing she had learned in the last few months: Enrico Chamberlain was not an easy man to understand. There were too many parts to him, too many sides to his character to figure out easily why he acted the way he did. How could he tell her he loved her and then drop her at the first sign of incriminating information without even listening to her explanation? Why had he so little trust in her?

It was too painful to think about and she pushed the thoughts away, taking another drink, feeling herself slide away into that dark feeling of dull misery.

'What are you going to do?' Dominique demanded.

'Do? There's nothing to do. I've tried talking to him and he won't listen. What else can I possibly do?'

'Put arsenic in his coffee.'

After dark that night, Chantal fled her room and its terrible, lonely silence, unable to cope with her own tears and despair. The room seemed to close in on her, suffocating her. She wanted to pound the walls, scream out her frustration, but it wasn't the sort of thing she ever did. She wished she could let go instead of clutching the pain inside, but she didn't know how.

She went to the beach and walked and walked, losing all sense of time. A sort of weary trance came over her as she listened to the monotonous pounding of the waves and gazed up at the endless dark sky stretched above. Endless ocean, endless sky, endless grief.

Her legs finally gave out and she dropped down in the sand, hugging her knees. She watched the waves as they washed on to the beach, foam and spume glowing eerily in the silvery moonlight.

Candles burned in hollows scooped out in the sand. She thought about Iemanjá, about good luck, about Enrico. She fingered the gold *figa* on the chain around her neck, her heart aching with sorrow. She struggled to her feet and walked into the water until it reached to her knees, staring out over the dark turbulent ocean.

Slowly she reached for the glasp of the chain and unfastened it. She felt the weight of the *figa* in her hand and she held on to it for a moment, feeling tears flow down her cheeks. Then, with one swift gesture, she flung the gold *figa* into the waves.

'For you, Iemanjá,' she whispered.

Actually, there was one thing left to do. Leave the Palácio, leave Rio.

Early the next morning, after an endless, sleepless night, she put a phone call through to the offices of the Bouchet Company in Paris.

'*Grand-père?* It's me, Chantal.' She settled back against the bed pillows and waited for the response on the other end of the line.

'Good. I've been waiting. What took you so long?'

'I didn't know you were waiting.'

'Of course I was waiting! I was hoping you'd come to your

senses and decide to do the right thing.'

'I've had a lot to think about.'

'One thing you'll have to learn is to make decisions faster. Indecision is not a good character trait for a businessperson.'

'I'll try and remember that.'

'So when are you coming?'

Chantal growned inwardly. Her grandfather was incorrigible. 'Who says I'm coming?'

'Of course you're coming! There was never any doubt, was there?'

Oh, yes there was, *Grand-père*! 'You know everything, don't you, *Grand-père*?'

He chuckled. 'I've got to. We're all ready for you here. You have your own office. It has been redecorated and we hired a secretary for you last week.'

She was speechless for a moment, then she decided to let it pass. 'I've made my reservations. I'll arrive in Paris on Tuesday.' She glanced at a typed itinerary in her hand and gave him the flight number and time of arrival.

'We'll send a car for you. You'll be staying at the apartment, of course.'

Of course. She made a face at the receiver, then smiled. Her grandfather was ready to take over her life, she could tell. For now she would let him. It didn't matter. And she would love to stay at her grandparents' elegant apartment on the Rue de Rivoli. It certainly would be easier for the time being.

'I'm looking forward to it, *Grand-père*.'

'So am I. But you'd better be prepared to work hard. Very hard.'

'Are you trying to scare me off?'

'Hah! You're not a weakling, are you?'

She laughed. 'I'll start taking my vitamins right now.'

'Good. See you Tuesday.' He hung up abruptly, as he

always did.

One day, she vowed, I'm going to beat him to it.

Paris in the winter must be the most depressing place in the world, Chantal thought, staring out of the limousine windows as the car drove through the wet, grey streets. The sky looked grey, the buildings looked grey. Everything was colourless and bare. The poeple looked pale and morose, huddling in their coats trying to hide from the rain and the world in general.

Making the change from the blistering summer heat of Rio de Janeiro to the miserable winter cold of Paris was not easy, and now, two weeks later, she still found herself always cold and always shivering despite the wool suits and coats.

She had spent a fortune buying winter clothes, mostly business suits and dresses, formal, but chic, to fit the conservative image of the Bouchet company.

She had never worked so hard in her life, or such long hours. The company had business dealings around the world, all linked to the Paris headquarters. Travel agencies, a small cargo airline, real-estate holdings all over Eurpoe and North Africa were only part of the assets. She was learning everything there was to learn, spending hours reading files and financial statements and reports. She found herself interested and absorbed. She studied acquisition proposals, financing strategies and marketing plans, asking many questions and preparing her own analysis and recommendations.

Her uncle and cousins had received her with reserved politeness, but not with hostility, which was a relief. She was determined to show them that she had good business sense despite the fact that she was of the female persuasion and had not graduated from the London School of Economics.

The limousine turned on to the Rue de Rivoli and came to a smooth stop in front of the apartment building a few minutes

later. The driver got out to open the door for her, his face
solemnly polite.

'*Merci*,' she said, as she climbed out. 'See you in the
morning.'

The weeks turned into months and Paris turned from grey to a
hesitant pale green, then suddenly burst into full spring.
Chantal sat in the company limousine with her grandmother
on the way to the airport to pick up Dominique and Nicole,
who were arriving from Rio. All four of them were to catch
another flight to Nice to spend a few relaxing days at the villa
on Cap d'Antibes.

They passed a small park with flower beds bright with
masses of sunny daffodils and Chantal smiled. Spring in Paris
was better, much better.

Her grandmother touched her hand. 'You don't smile
much, *chérie*. You're so beautiful when you smile.'

Chantal gently squeezed the frail, wrinkled hand in reply.
There hadn't been much to smile about the last few months.
No matter how much she worked, how many hours of the day,
thoughts of Enrico always haunted her. Every time she entered
a crowded room, she searched for his face. She didn't know
why she was looking for him here, in Paris, but she was always
looking.

'A few days at the villa will do you good,' her grandmother
was saying. 'You work too hard, you know.'

'I enjoy my work, *Grand-mère*. I even get along with *Grand-père*. Who ever expected that?'

She was looking forward to seeing Dominique and Nicole. It
would be wonderful just to laze around for a while and talk
and go to the beach with Nicole. A memory stirred and she felt
a flash of pain. Nicole and Enrico at the Ipanema beach,
playing with a yellow plastic bottle. Memories would always

be there. She would have to learn to live with them.

Live. Sometimes she felt as if she weren't fully alive, as if she were merely going through the motions. She was afraid to feel anything, afraid if she let herself feel, she wouldn't be able to bear the pain.

'He left Rio, didn't you know?'

Dominique, in a minuscule white bikini, sat on a lounger on the terrace of the villa, sipping a glass of Perrier.

'I didn't know,' Chantal said tonelessly. Her mother never mentioned Enrico in their telephone conversations and Chantal didn't ask.

'He's running the Hotel Principado in Madrid. It's supposed to be absolutely gorgeous. I saw the promotional material with the pictures.'

'I thought Uncle Matteus already had a GM to run it.

Dominique waved her hand. 'Something happened. He had a heart attack or something,' she said casually.

'I see.' Chantal took a swallow of lemonade. 'How's Bernard?' she asked.

'Fine. He asked me to marry him.'

'And what did you say?'

'I said never.'

'Did you really?'

Dominique gave a half-smile. 'No. I said I wasn't ready to think about it yet.'

'You're afraid?'

'No.' Dominique clinked the ice in her glass. 'Terrified.'

'So what did Bernard say?'

'He said he'll un-terrify me.'

Chantal laughed. 'I hope so.' She surveyed the garden with its profusion of flowering bushes. It was beautiful restful place, and very quiet apart from the chirping of the birds and the buzzing of insects. At the far left she could see the sparkle of the sky-blue pool, its irregular shape designed to fit the natural contours of the landscape.'

Dominique sat straight up and deposited her empty glass on a small table. She galnced over at Chantal. 'You really did love him, didn't you?'

Chantal bit her lip. 'Yes.'

'You look terrible. You look as if you're only half alive. It isn't the work, is it?'

Chantal shrugged, saying nothing.

Dominique sighed. 'God, I wish I could have done something.'

'It's not you fault.'

'I know. It's just . . . I don't know.' She waved her hand helplessly. 'You didn't deserve it, Chantal.'

Chantal closed her eyes briefly. 'The worst of it was that he didn't believe me.' Her voice shook and suddenly tears burned behind her eyelids. She swallowed hard. 'Oh, damn!' she muttered, and came to her feet. 'I'm going for a swim.'

Dominique didn't mention Enrico again and Chantal was grateful. It was a happy weekeend and it was joy to watch little Nicole charm her great-grandparents.

She was sorry to return to Paris, but the three days off had refreshed her and she went back to work with renewed energy.

Two weeks later she received a postcard from Dominique sent from Athens where she was visitng a friend. 'Having a wonderful time here. This place is great. We should tell Uncle M to buy or build a hotel here. Or does he have one here already? I haven't talked to him for a week.'

Chantal laughed. In the last several months, Uncle Matteus had acquired two more hotels—one in Rome and another in Rabat, Morocco. 'He's not going to stop,' Dominique had said, 'until he has one in every country on the globe.'

Smiling, Chantal put the card aside and sorted through the rest of her morning's mail. Reports and letters and telexes from half a dozen places around the world. It was amazing how far the Bouchet Company's business dealings reached. There were several memos and a few telexes as well. She glanced at them quickly, her eyes suddenly catching a name that made her heart jump into her throat. *Hotel Principado, Madrid.*

She grew very still, so still she even forgot to breathe. Her eyes were transfixed on the paper and her heart raced with frantic speed.

It was a telex directed to her personally, and it was signed 'ENRICO.'

CHAPTER TEN

'PLEASE MEET ME IN MADRID.'

That was all. Her hand shook so badly, the paper slipped from her fingers and fluttered to the floor. Throat dry, heart racing she stared unseeingly out the window.'

He wanted to meet her.

Why? What did he want from her now? There was no explanation, no indication at all on the telex. If he wanted to see her, why didn't he come to Paris?

Damn you! she muttered and pushed her chair back with so much force it almost tipped over. She got up and walked to the window, her legs unsteady.

She knew that secretly she was always hoping to see him, to look into the cool grey eyes unexpectedly across some crowded room. At the airport a few weeks ago, she had looked around, wishing, hoping to see his face. It was crazy, insane, but she couldn't help herself. She knew her life was in some sort of holding pattern because she hadn't yet given up, could never give up hope that Enrico would come back to her. She hadn't wanted to admit this, burying herself in work, trying to forget him. Of course she had not succeeded.

She had dreamed of seeing him again, but she had never expected a telex, a cold white piece of paper with a simple message in black letters—'PLEASE MEET ME IN MADRID.'

Her hands clenched into fists. If he wants to see me, let him come to Paris, she thought furiously, not knowing why she was suddenly so angry. Who does he think he is to make me do the walking? I am not one of his employees he can summon at his own convenience! I have work to do! I am busy!

She worked herself into a rage, turned away abruptly from the window and sat back down in her chair just as the telphone rang.

There was no more time to ponder the telex for the rest of the day. She blocked it out forcefully, concentrating on her work. There were meetings, a business lunch with her grandfather and a London lawyer, telephone calls to make, and an endless number of other things to tend to. She took work home with her and sat until all hours of the night poring over piles of papers until she could barely keep her eyes open.

Her body ached, her head throbbed, her stomach cramped with anxiety.

She went to bed and couldn't sleep. She knew why she had been so angry when she had received the telex. It wasn't really anger she was feeling. It was fear. She was terrified.

Let him come to Paris. I have work to do. I am too busy. They were just excuses. If she truly loved him, then there was not place for wounded pride. He had taken the first step: 'PLEASE MEET ME IN MADRID.' And he *had* said please, hadn't he?

The flight from Paris to Madrid took two hours and seven minutes. It might as well have been a year. She was too nervous to eat or drink the lavish dinner given her in the first-class section, which was nearly emtpy.

She had not made a reservation at the Principado, nor called or telexed Enrico to let him know she was coming. Somewhere in the back of her mind she wanted an escape. If at the last minute she decided she didn't want to see him she could turn right back and he would never know about it. She was fooling herself, she knew full well. She was frightened and nervous, but there was nothing she wanted more than to see Enrico again.

There was hope and she had to hold on to it. Yet there were so many unanswered questions. Why had he suddenly contacted her after all these months? What was the real reason he wanted to see her? Could there be something else besides their personal relationship or lack thereof?

She couldn't think what it could possibly be. She couldn't think at all. Her mind was in a turmoil and her stomach felt as if she had swallowed wet cement.

She sat silently in the back of the taxi as it drove her to the Hotel Principado. It was still light, a humid, hot summer's evening with people everywhere in the streets, sitting on pavement cafés drinking wine and eating dinner or drinking coffee. It was a lively city, but she had no eye for the happenings outisde.

The Principado was impressive—a beautiful, centuries-old building in the centre of town. Completely restored now, it had a regal façade and a prominent entrance.

She paid the driver and followed the doorman, resplendent in a red and gold uniform, into the hotel lobby. She had only a small overnight bag and she carried it up to the desk herself.

'I would like a room, please.'

She filled in a form and produced a credit card, then waited until the information was typed into the computer. Moments later she was following a skinny, dark-eyed bellhop into a lift and down a corridor. He opened the door for her, turned on the lights and opened the connecting door into the bedroom.

'I asked for a room,' she said, frowning. 'I don't need a suite.'

'This is the Rio Suite, *senorita*,' he said. 'It's for certain guests only. We have a standing reservation for you.'

'All right, *gracias*.' She was in no mood to argue about it at this time.

The décor of the suite was opulent, but she only glanced at it quickly, not taking in any details. There was a more important matter on her mind.

She took a deep breath, trying to steady her nerves. What should she do now? Call the desk and ask them to connect her with Enrico's apartment? And then what? Say, Hello Enrico, I'm here. You wanted me to come and I came like a good little girl.

She pressed her eye shut and rubbed her neck. God, she was nervous. She took a deep breath and exhaled slowly.

A knock on the door almost made her jump. Good God, what was the matter with her?

She opened the door, expecting a maid, the bellhop. She wasn't expecting Enrico.

Her heart lurched and her throat went dry. She stared at him speechlessly, unable to utter a sound.

'Hello, Chantal,' he said quietly. 'May I come in?'

Silently she stepped aside to let him pass, still not trusting her voice. He was wearing casual white trousers and a blue, shot-sleeved shirt. He was as tall and handsome as ever, yet he looked different. He was thinner and she noticed for the first time a streak of grey in his dark hair. He looked older than she remembered, with a dull weariness in the grey eyes.

Grey eyes that looked into hers, eyes that made her nerves jump as the silence vibrated between them.

'You came,' he said softly, as if he couldn't quite believe it.

She swallowed. 'What else could I possibly do?' She knew she gave herself away with those words, but she couldn't help it. Her love for him was like a deep ache and it hurt to stand there with this terrible chasm of pain and mistrust separating them.

'You could have ignored it.'

She shook her head. I loved you. I still love you, she wanted to say, but she knew if she voiced the words she would start to cry.

He pushed his hands into his pockets. He seemed, for a moment, lost for words. 'I understand you're making yourself indispensable in Paris.'

'I enjoy the challenge.'

'No licking of stamps?'

She shook her head, managing a small smile. Her muscles seeemd stiff, unyielding. 'No.'

He glanced at her pale summer suit. 'You look very . . . businesslike. Elegant, but rather formal. I don't know you this way.'

No, he didn't. He had seen her dressed in causal beach-wear or chic designer evening clothes, not in a prim skirt and jacket with her hair coiled soberly on top of her head. 'I went to the airport straight from the office. I haven't had a chance to change.'

They were making meaningless small talk to fill the awkward void between them. She tucked a stray strand of hair behind her ear. 'I din't know you'd left Rio,' she said. 'Dominique told me you were in Madrid.'

'It's only for a year, probably, to get the place going.'

'You like Madrid?'

He shrugged lightly. 'It's fine. It doesn't really matter so much where I am.'

No, she thought, it isn't the place that counts. He has no moorings, like me. No real roots, She studied his face and he turned away from her as if he didn't want her to read his feelings in his eyes. He's lonely, she thought. He's been so lonely for such a long time.

He stared out of the window, his back to her, stress visible in every rigid line and angle of the tall body. Madrid sparkled in the dark, bright-coloured city lights taunting the night. Silence hung in the room, palpable, unnerving. Slowly, he turned and faced her.

'Chantal, you once asked me to listen to you and I refused.' His eyes held hers and she felt the nervous fluttering of her heart. 'I am now asking you if you will please listen to me.'

He knew she had every right to refuse but she had not come all the way here to do that. He watched her intently, face taut with strain, waiting for her reply.

She nodded. 'I'll listen.'

He thrust a hand through his hair. 'Here? Now? I didn't even give you a chance to settle in. Have you had dinner yet?'

'Here and now is fine and I don't want to eat.' If she had to wait any more for this conversation she would crack under the tension. She kicked off her shoes and sat down in a chair. Her suit was not made for lounging, but it was not an important consideration at the moment.

He gazed down at her, frowning. 'Why don't you get out of that damn career-woman outfit,' he suggested. He gave a lopsided grin. 'I know I'm being unreasonable, but I feel as if I'm talking to a stranger.'

He was uneasy, she knew. He found it difficult to talk to her. It was an amazing revelation to see him so uncertain. She came to her feet. 'Sure.' She went into the bedroom and closed the door. She let out a deep sigh, suddenly aware of the tautness of her body.

It took her only minutes to change into some casual blue slacks and a flowered silk shirt. She took the pins out of her hair and shook it loose. She stared at herself in the mirror, shocked for the first time in months at the hollow look of her face, the emptiness in the green eyes. She applied some blush on her cheeks and brushed out her hair.

Enrico was mixing himself a drink from the small bar when

she came back into the room.

'Do you want one?' he asked.

'A glass of red wine, please.'

'It'll have to be Spanish,' he said with mock apology. 'No Brazilian here.'

She gave a half-smile. 'I'll suffer through it.'

He handed her the glass, his eyes skimming over her. 'That's better. Thank you.' He sat down in a chair across from her and took a slow drink from his glass. The ice tinkled. Chantal watched him, waiting. She tried to read his face, but it was difficult to guess what emotions lay behind the tightly controlled façade of his face.

'I thought you were perfect,' he said unsteadily. 'The most perfect woman I'd ever met.'

It wasn't what she had expected to hear and she gave him a startled look. There was a strange, unreadable expression on his face and his eyes seemed focused on some inner vision.

'You were sensitive and caring and loving,' he went on. 'You had integrity and loyalty and no pretensions. You were beautiful.' He took another drink from his glass, and gave a crooked smile.

'I didn't see that right from the beginning, as I'm sure you remember. I fell in love with you little by little. I fell in love with you listening to your music, seeing your face as you talked about your father, watching you with my sister. You were a real person. You liked my nutty sister. You were not the spoiled little rich girl I had expected you to be.' He paused, his eyes cloudy. 'It was the first big mistake I made—assuming you would be like the other women I knew—selfish and shallow. But you were not like that. You were so different. You were everything I could possibly want in a woman.'

There was a long silence and Chantal could feel the nervous anxiety growing inside her. She watched him, seeing the emotions in his eyes, his face painfully taut. She noticed his hands, clenching and unclenching.

He straightened in his chair and looked right at her, then closed his eyes briefly as if it were too difficult to speak while he saw her face. 'Then I got that report from the investigators and that whole perfect image of you shattered.' His voice was husky and strained. He swallowed visibly. 'You'd had an affair with a married man. You'd broken up a marriage and driven a woman to become a mental patient. I thought of this Amanda and all I could see was the memory of my mother when I was fifteen.'

'*Your mother?*' she whispered.

'When she found out my father had had a mistress for three years, kept her in a luxury apartment, spent thousand of dollars on her, taken her on expensive trips and had gone into debt to pay for it all. And my mother was working as a maid in the Marriott to keep us going. That's when she broke down and accepted my grandfather's offer to pay for our tickets back to Brazil. She could deal with gambling debts; she couldn't deal with his infidelity.' He paused. 'I shall never forget her face the day she found out about my father's mistress.'

She saw the raw pain in his face and it was all clear to her now, so very clear. She swallowed at the constriction in her throat.

'I'm sorry,' she said.

'I'm the one to be sorry. My memory clouded all reality. It made me blind and deaf to you. It overwhelmed my trust in you. In my mind you done to Amanda what my father and his mistress had done to my mother. All I could see were the outside facts and I judged you without thinking further.   I didn't believe you.' His voice shook. 'I couldn't.'

But did he now? And why, after all these months?

'And now?' Her voice was low, as if she were afraid to ask

the question.

He closed his eyes briefly. 'Chantal, I don't know how to ask you to forgive me. I don't know how I am ever going to forgive myself. What I did to you . . . accuse you, not believe you, not even listen to you . . . such a terrible lack of trust . . .' His words struggled to a stop. Fear and despair darkened his eyes. 'I only hope it isn't too late.'

Tears misted her vision and her throat closed up. She couldn't speak.

He rubbed his forehead as if to ease the tension. 'I didn't come to Paris to see you because I didn't think I could bear the rejection if you didn't want me any more. I sent that telex asking you to come here, so that if you did come, I would know you still cared enough to talk to me.'

She swallowed hard. Her mouth trembled. 'I never stopped caring, Enrico. It's not too late.' Her voice was a husky whisper and she tried with all her might not to let the tears spill over.

He stared at her, grey eyes suddenly alight with hope.

She moistened her lips.

'I love you,' she said softly.

His face contorted and his mouth worked. He leaped out his chair and knelt in front of her and scooped her into his arms. 'Oh, God, Chantal,' he groaned. 'Tell me again. Say it again.'

'I love you.' And then the tears did flow over and she wept against his shirt, shedding tears for all the pain of the last months, tears of relief and hope.

'I love you,' he whispered fiercely. 'I love you. I have never loved anybody the way I love you. I've been insane to let this happen to us. I haven't been alive these last few months.' He kissed her eyes, her mouth. 'Don't cry, please don't cry.'

'I'm sorry, I'm sorry.'

He held her against him and stroked her hair until she calmed down. She blew her nose and wiped her eyes.

'Sorry. I must look awful.'

'You look wonderful. You're here, in my arms. Oh, God, I

was terrified I had lost you. When I finally came to my senses I was going mad with remorse and fear. Hold me, kiss me.'

They held each other like drowning victims, kissing hungrily, eagerly, until finally, breathlessly, they drew apart. She gave a shaky laugh. 'You've never kissed me like that before.'

'It did lack a certain finesse,' he admitted, humour in his voice. 'I'll work on finesse when I've calmed down.'

'I wasn't complaining.' She laid her cheek against his. 'What made you change your mind? Why did you suddenly decide you wanted to see me?'

'He sighed heavily. 'I'd been living in some sort of stupor ever since I received that report about Amanda. Somebody shook me out of it. Somebody finally got though to me and made me see the truth.'

She pulled away from his so that she could see his face. 'Who?' Who could possibly have done that?

His mouth quirked. 'You're not going to believe this. It was Dominique.'

'*Dominique?*' She shook her head in utter amazement. 'Dominique doesn't want to be in the same *city* with you! When did you see her? Where?'

'She made an appoinment with my secretary last week to see me in my office here in the hotel.'

Last week. That must have been after she had left Cap d'Antibes, before she went to Athens to see her friend.

'I can't believe she did this,' she whispered. 'That she came to Madrid to see you. She hates you.'

'But she loves you,' he said drily. 'She did it for you. It took a lot of guts and I admire her for that.'

He would. He admired guts and loyalty.

'She came in here, all haughty and full of indignant fury. She said she didn't give a damn what I thought about her, but she was going to make me listen to her if it was the last thing she did. I hadn't wanted to listen to you, but I was damn well going to listen to her.'

'So you did?'

'I did.' A funny little smile tugged at his mouth. 'You're sister is a rather interesting person. She quite surprised me, I have to admit. I couldn't believe she'd come to Madrid to see me. She told me the whole story about you and David. She shook me out of my stupor, brought me to my senses. That's the only way I can explain it. I know now that something had to happen, that I couldn't go on the way I had been living since you left. Subconsciously, I was waiting for someting to happen, but I never would have expected it to be Dominique.'

'Maybe she isn't quite as selfish and shallow as you take her for.'

One corner of his mouth turned up. 'Maybe there are a few redeeming qualities. Maybe I shouldn't judge people quite so harshly. I'm not exactly perfect myself.'

'Sshh.' She touched a finger to his lips. 'Let's not talk any more.'

'But I'm not finished.'

'I don't want to hear any more tales of woe. I've had enough. I want to forget everything. I want to be happy.'

'Would marrying me make you happy?'

'No,' she whispered. 'It would make me ecstatic.'

'Ecstatic is good. Ecstatic is great.'

She leaned agianst him and sighed. 'How are we going to do this? I live in Paris and you live in Madrid. I can't give up my work. Not now. I'm committed. You understand that, don't you?'

He kissed her gently on the mouth. 'All I ask is that you don't wear those career suits when I'm around. Madrid to Paris is only a two-hour flight. We can spend the weekends together. Or we can buy a house somewhere near Nice and split the distance. I won't be here more than a year and I'll be quite ready for a hotel in Paris.'

'Uncle Matteus doesn't have a hotel in Paris.'

'Not as of today, you're right.' He kissed her. 'Now stop talking, woman.'

She sighed and closed her eyes. '*Sim, senhor.*'

'That's Portuguese,' he whispered, unbuttoning her shirt. 'We're in Spain.'

'*Oui, monsieur.*'

'That's French. Don't you know your language?' He unclasped her bra and kissed her breasts with tantalising little kisses, his tongue teasing.

'Oh, be quiet,' she moaned. 'How can you expect me to think straight at a time like this?' She lifted his face between her hands and kissed him. 'I love you,' she murmured against his lips. '*Je t'aime, te amo, eu te amo, ich liebe dich.* That's English, French, Spanish, Portuguese and German—in that order. How's that?'

'Better, much better. I didn't know you spoke German.'

'One summer, when I was sixteen, I had a German boyfriend.'

He groaned. 'Don't tell me about it, please.'

She laughed softly. 'I wasn't going to.'

Have You Ever Wondered If You Could Write A Harlequin Novel?

Here's great news—Harlequin is offering a series of cassette tapes to help you do just that. Written by Harlequin editors, these tapes give practical advice on how to make your characters—and your story—come alive. There's a tape for each contemporary romance series Harlequin publishes.

Mail order only

All sales final

INDULGE A LITTLE SWEEPSTAKES

OFFICIAL RULES

SWEEPSTAKES RULES AND REGULATIONS. NO PURCHASE NECESSARY.

1. NO PURCHASE NECESSARY. To enter complete the official entry form and return with the invoice in the envelope provided. Or you may enter by printing your name, complete address and your daytime phone number on a 3 x 5 piece of paper. Include with your entry the hand printed words "Indulge A Little Sweepstakes." Mail your entry to: Indulge A Little Sweepstakes, P.O. Box 1397, Buffalo, NY 14269-1397. No mechanically reproduced entries accepted. Not responsible for late, lost, misdirected mail, or printing errors.

2. Three winners, one per month (Sept. 30, 1989, October 31, 1989 and November 30, 1989), will be selected in random drawings. All entries received prior to the drawing date will be eligible for that month's prize. This sweepstakes is under the supervision of MARDEN-KANE, INC. an independent judging organization whose decisions are final and binding. Winners will be notified by telephone and may be required to execute an affidavit of eligibility and release which must be returned within 14 days, or an alternate winner will be selected.

3. Prizes: 1st Grand Prize (1) a trip for two to Disneyworld in Orlando, Florida. Trip includes round trip air transportation, hotel accommodations for seven days and six nights, plus up to $700 expense money (ARV $3,500). 2nd Grand Prize (1) a seven-night Chandris Caribbean Cruise for two includes transportation from nearest major airport, accommodations, meals plus up to $1,000 in expense money (ARV $4,300). 3rd Grand Prize (1) a ten-day Hawaiian holiday for two includes round trip air transportation for two, hotel accommodations, sightseeing, plus up to $1,200 in spending money (ARV $7,700). All trips subject to availability and must be taken as outlined on the entry form.

4. Sweepstakes open to residents of the U.S. and Canada 18 years or older except employees and the families of Torstar Corp., its affiliates, subsidiaries and Marden-Kane, Inc. and all other agencies and persons connected with conducting this sweepstakes. All Federal, State and local laws and regulations apply. Void wherever prohibited or restricted by law. Taxes, if any are the sole responsibility of the prize winners. Canadian winners will be required to answer a skill testing question. Winners consent to the use of their name, photograph and/or likeness for publicity purposes without additional compensation.

5. For a list of prize winners, send a stamped, self-addressed envelope to Indulge A Little Sweepstakes Winners, P.O. Box 701, Sayreville, NJ 08871.

© 1989 HARLEQUIN ENTERPRISES LTD.   DL-SWPS

INDULGE A LITTLE SWEEPSTAKES

OFFICIAL RULES

SWEEPSTAKES RULES AND REGULATIONS. NO PURCHASE NECESSARY.

1. NO PURCHASE NECESSARY. To enter complete the official entry form and return with the invoice in the envelope provided. Or you may enter by printing your name, complete address and your daytime phone number on a 3 x 5 piece of paper. Include with your entry the hand printed words "Indulge A Little Sweepstakes." Mail your entry to: Indulge A Little Sweepstakes, P.O. Box 1397, Buffalo, NY 14269-1397. No mechanically reproduced entries accepted. Not responsible for late, lost, misdirected mail, or printing errors.

2. Three winners, one per month (Sept. 30, 1989, October 31, 1989 and November 30, 1989), will be selected in random drawings. All entries received prior to the drawing date will be eligible for that month's prize. This sweepstakes is under the supervision of MARDEN-KANE, INC. an independent judging organization whose decisions are final and binding. Winners will be notified by telephone and may be required to execute an affidavit of eligibility and release which must be returned within 14 days, or an alternate winner will be selected.

3. Prizes: 1st Grand Prize (1) a trip for two to Disneyworld in Orlando, Florida. Trip includes round trip air transportation, hotel accommodations for seven days and six nights, plus up to $700 expense money (ARV $3,500). 2nd Grand Prize (1) a seven-night Chandris Caribbean Cruise for two includes transportation from nearest major airport, accommodations, meals plus up to $1,000 in expense money (ARV $4,300). 3rd Grand Prize (1) a ten-day Hawaiian holiday for two includes round trip air transportation for two, hotel accommodations, sightseeing, plus up to $1,200 in spending money (ARV $7,700). All trips subject to availability and must be taken as outlined on the entry form.

4. Sweepstakes open to residents of the U.S. and Canada 18 years or older except employees and the families of Torstar Corp., its affiliates, subsidiaries and Marden-Kane, Inc. and all other agencies and persons connected with conducting this sweepstakes. All Federal, State and local laws and regulations apply. Void wherever prohibited or restricted by law. Taxes, if any are the sole responsibility of the prize winners. Canadian winners will be required to answer a skill testing question. Winners consent to the use of their name, photograph and/or likeness for publicity purposes without additional compensation.

5. For a list of prize winners, send a stamped, self-addressed envelope to Indulge A Little Sweepstakes Winners, P.O. Box 701, Sayreville, NJ 08871.

© 1989 HARLEQUIN ENTERPRISES LTD.   DL-SWPS

INDULGE A LITTLE—WIN A LOT!

Summer of '89 Subscribers-Only Sweepstakes

OFFICIAL ENTRY FORM

This entry must be received by: October 31, 1989
This month's winner will be notified by: Nov. 7, 1989
Trip must be taken between: Dec. 7, 1989–April 7, 1990
(depending on sailing schedule)

YES, I want to win the Caribbean cruise vacation for two! I understand the prize includes round-trip airfare, a one-week cruise including private cabin and all meals, and a daily allowance as revealed on the "Wallet" scratch-off card.

Name_____

Address_____

City_____ State/Prov._____ Zip/Postal Code_____

Daytime phone number _____
                              Area code

Return entries with invoice in envelope provided. Each book in this shipment has two entry coupons—and the more coupons you enter, the better your chances of winning!

© 1989 HARLEQUIN ENTERPRISES LTD.

DINDL-2

INDULGE A LITTLE—WIN A LOT!

Summer of '89 Subscribers-Only Sweepstakes

OFFICIAL ENTRY FORM

This entry must be received by: October 31, 1989
This month's winner will be notified by: Nov. 7, 1989
Trip must be taken between: Dec. 7, 1989–April 7, 1990
(depending on sailing schedule)

YES, I want to win the Caribbean cruise vacation for two! I understand the prize includes round-trip airfare, a one-week cruise including private cabin and all meals, and a daily allowance as revealed on the "Wallet" scratch-off card.

Name_____

Address_____

City_____ State/Prov._____ Zip/Postal Code_____

Daytime phone number _____
                              Area code

Return entries with invoice in envelope provided. Each book in this shipment has two entry coupons—and the more coupons you enter, the better your chances of winning!

© 1989 HARLEQUIN ENTERPRISES LTD.

DINDL-2